MW01074195

Into the Dark

A Post Apocalyptic Adventure

Kevin Partner

Scribbleit

Copyright © 2022 by Kevin Partner

All rights reserved.

No part of this publication may be reproduced, distributed, or trans-mitted in any form or by any means, including photocopying, record-ing, or other electronic or mechanical methods, without the prior written permission of the publisher, except as permitted by U.S. copyright law. For permission requests, contact [include publish-er/author contact info].

The story, all names, characters, and incidents portrayed in this production are fictitious. No identification with actual persons (living or deceased), places, buildings, and products is intended or should be inferred.

Book Cover by GetCovers.com

CONTENTS

THE STORY SO FAR

Thirty-five years after the end of the world, Reuben Bane, former Foundation exciser, seeks to redeem himself by fulfilling a promise made to the man who saved him from the plague. Having rescued Asha, a mysterious deviant child, and allowed a young, naive man called Skeeter to ride with them, they have escaped the vengeful pursuit of the local sheriff and can now head east. How soon will it be before they ride into trouble?

Hannah Myers survived the double apocalypse and eventually settled in West Virginia where she became a trusted city councilor, continuing her career as a scientist as she seeks to preserve some of the knowledge that will be lost with her generation. Having been forced to agree to the banishment of a good man, she fears for her mutant son when the Foundation comes to town.

Zak Archer is a young servant of the Foundation, waiting on one of the nine Shepherds. His life was harsh but simple enough, until Father Ruiz introduced him to the beautiful Eve, who is to be the mother of a new generation of genetically perfect people — the inheritors of paradise. Now he must become her protector, on Ruiz's orders while obeying the command of his mentor, Mr. Wong: don't fall in love with her.

Chapter 1

BRIGANDS

REUBEN PULLED LUCIFER TO a halt and waited as the horse fidgeted.

"Who'd you figure they are?" Skeeter asked, drawing alongside and pulling the shotgun from behind his saddle. "Bandits?"

Reuben shrugged, trying to appear unconcerned when, in fact, he was seething at his own carelessness. It was a warm, late spring afternoon and they'd been riding at ease. It had been a week since they'd escaped from Flowood, and his main concern was finding somewhere to camp and build a fire. He'd brought down a young deer before they'd set out that morning. Its carcass was tied to Lucifer's back, and the thought of his first good meal since he'd left Jackson had dulled his instincts. It had been Asha who'd called out that there were men riding down the highway toward them.

How he'd seen them first, given that he was a boy on a small pony, and was half asleep at the time, was a mystery for another day. There was something odd about Asha that Reuben couldn't quite put his finger on.

"Just be calm and leave the talking to me," he said to both of his companions. "Not everyone on the road is a threat, but bandits come in many forms."

There were three of them, all men, riding in a relaxed fashion, hooves clopping along the cracked and broken surface of the highway. They were dressed similarly; wide-brimmed hats and light cotton jackets with long rifles hanging down from their saddles, and revolvers at their hips. Each had a square of yellow cloth pinned to his shoulder with a star embroidered on it.

Reuben's Colt 1911 was visible on his belt, but he kept his hands on Lucifer's reins, his fingers relaxed.

"Yo, stranger," the first man said as he halted ten feet away. "Name's Woodward. Care to state your business?"

"I do not. My business is my own affair."

Woodward — a blue-eyed man in his thirties with a well-tended flaxen beard and a long, white scar beneath his eye — couldn't conceal his surprise. So, he was used to easy intimidation. "These are the lands of Mr. Gabriel Simmons, and no one travels here without his say so."

"Where is this Simmons?"

"*Mister* Simmons is likely at his ranch, but his rangers watch the roads and keep the peace. Now, why don't you tell me where you're headed? I'm sure you don't want trouble."

Reuben sighed and weighed up the man with his eyes. A capable fighter, he judged, probably quick enough on the draw to pose a threat, though used to getting his way by bullying rather than resorting to violence, in general.

Nudging Lucifer a couple of steps forward, Reuben lifted his head so the sun illuminated his face.

"Hey, what the hell is that on your face? You got the plague?" Woodward held out his hand, palm away from him as if to keep Reuben away. His companions edged backwards.

"I had it a year ago. My name is Reuben Bane," he said, watching Woodward closely, but seeing no sign of recognition, "and this is Skeeter and Asha, who are travelling with me."

Woodward's eyes narrowed as he very obviously stared at Reuben's pock-marked chin.

"You ain't infected anymore?"

"Like I said, I had it a year ago. Nearly killed me."

He nodded. "Where you headed?"

"North and east."

"Place got a name?"

"It has, but I do not wish my movements to be followed."

Woodward rubbed his bearded chin. "Beyond Greene County?"

"Far beyond."

Glancing at his comrades, Woodward thought for a moment, then grunted. "You'll stick to the highway."

"We'll camp beside it, but our direct route is this way."

"Okay. But take some advice, will you?"

"I'm listening."

"Mr. Simmons don't appreciate no interference in his affairs, so I suggest you pass through as quick as you can and keep yourselves to yourselves."

"What does he have to hide?"

Woodward shook his head, his voice becoming animated. "He ain't got nothin' to hide. This county is peaceful, and we don't tolerate no brigands, but these are harsh times and justice is pretty quick and pretty final. The folks who live here give thanks for the peace, and they don't take kindly to wanderers. My advice is to keep your heads down and get out of the county as quick as possible. Not all the other rangers are as trusting as me."

The man on the horse behind Woodward moved forward and pointed at Lucifer's back before whispering something into the ranger's ear. Woodward nodded.

"You shot a deer, I see."

Reuben's heart sank. "You are welcome to a leg."

"All game in this county belongs to Mr. Simmons, so we'll be confiscating this," Woodward said. Then, seeing Reuben's expression, he added, "Poaching's a hangin' offense, but we'll look the other way if you're cooperative."

AFTER A CHEERLESS, HUNGRY camp under an unremitting drizzle, the three weary travelers emerged from the tree-lined highway to an open countryside. The road wound its way down a gentle slope, running between patches of woodland in a landscape so green it made the eye ache for a different color. Anything other than the gray of the sky, that is.

Reuben felt his heart lift at the vast open space after the confines of the tree-lined road. Here, the new trees that had sprung up since the devastation of thirty-five years before had been cleared and used to build the cabins that dotted the rectangular pattern of fields.

His spirits rose and then fell as the wind whipped up the valley, bringing more rain and making him feel exposed. He longed for a real bed to sleep in, even if only for one night. Preferably with a roof over it. And a warm meal in his belly. Then he could attend to the bandage on his forearm. The pain had diminished to a background ache, but the skin was warm around it and he needed to replace the dressing. For that, he needed a fire to boil water over.

Reuben looked over his shoulder to see Skeeter leaning wearily on his pommel, the rain running down his hat. Next to him, Asha made for an even more pathetic figure. He wore Reuben's traveling cloak, but wasn't equipped for any kind of journey. He needed rest, warmth and food. But he wasn't going to get it here.

There was no doubt in Reuben's mind that Woodward's warning was a genuine one. If they were found wandering in land claimed by the mysterious Mr. Simmons, their punishment would be swift and final.

But they needed shelter. The trick, then, was to make sure they weren't seen.

Skeeter raised himself when he noticed that they'd stopped and forced a smile. "I don't think much of this weather for travelin', boss. Give good money for a square meal and somewhere to sleep."

"Have you got any money?"

"Good point. I guess I forgot to bring my pocketbook with me."

Reuben chuckled and nudged Lucifer into a slow walk, but stopped when he noticed that Asha wasn't following. "You okay, boy?"

He got no answer, and Skeeter leaned over to touch Asha's face. "He's awful cold, Mr. Reuben."

Bane could see the boy shivering, so he climbed off Lucifer's back and walked to stand by Blossom's stirrups. "Asha, can you hear me?"

"He ain't got the plague, has he?"

"Don't be a fool!" Reuben said, shooting a venomous look at Skeeter. "Can you see any swellings? Plague burns you up."

Skeeter must have lived a miserable life, Reuben reflected, to be so impervious to insult. He merely shrugged and put his hand on Asha's shoulder. "Well, he's sick, that's for sure and certain. We got to find him somewhere to rest up, or I don't reckon he'll make it."

Reuben felt the boy's forehead. Cold and clammy, but likely the prelude to much worse. Not the plague, but it might as well be. He cursed under his breath in frustration. He had a mission. He'd been told to find the woman by the end of the spring, and that wasn't far away. Once that was done, he'd be free to go off and die once he'd had his revenge on the Foundation. Hannah Myers, however, was still the best part of a thousand miles away, but each time he thought he'd be able to make good progress, something happened to stop him. Generally speaking, something to do with this child. He should leave the boy and carry on.

But he wouldn't. That wasn't who he was anymore. His old self would have said he'd become weak in his dotage, and that was certainly true.

Better to be weak than the man he once was, however.

He lifted Asha off Blossom's saddle, marveling at how light he was. When they'd first met, he'd guessed Asha to be no more than thirteen years old, but now he seemed much younger. Skeeter held the boy on Lucifer's saddle as Reuben climbed up and wrapped his arms around Asha and took the reins.

"Come on," he said to Skeeter. "Warning or no, we'll have to find somewhere to shelter, and quick."

"I got you, boss," the younger man said, before vaulting into the saddle in a sickeningly nimble fashion and urging his mount forward along the highway.

In Reuben's arms, Asha groaned and then drifted off into unconsciousness.

Chapter 2

HANNAH

"ANY SIGN OF HIM?" Mitch Snider whispered as he marched alongside Hannah toward city hall.

"No. It's been a week and I keep expecting to hear about some freak being cornered and shot."

Hannah's eyes looked all around, looking for figures hidden in shadows. She'd barely had a moment to talk with Snider since the Foundation had pounced on the city of Mecklen and she already missed the freedom they'd taken for granted. For all his slipperiness, Mayor Mitch Snider was an ally, and she'd take him as a governor over Carver, the man who now held power here.

Mitch grabbed her arm as she stumbled.

"Thanks."

"Have you had any sleep? You look half dead."

"If they find Roberto, I'll be one hundred percent dead," she said, forcing a smile. "And no, I can't sleep. The place is too quiet without him there."

"If the Foundation had found him, I'm pretty sure we'd know about it already."

That was the only crumb of comfort she could find. But she couldn't move past the thought of Roberto, her mutant son, alone and afraid, hiding somewhere like some monster in the woods.

The Foundation flag hung limp on the pole outside city hall, and they climbed the steps to meet Ida Beale who'd been lurking outside the door.

"Don't wanna go in there on my own," the old woman said. "Fella gives me the creeps." She forced a smile, but the strain was obvious. Then she raised one eyebrow, asking the silent question, sighing as Hannah shook her head.

Carver was already in place at the head of the council table. Hannah shot a glance at Mitch who stiffened as he saw the man in his former seat. Officially, Mitch was still in charge, but Carver and his colleagues had made it clear that any authority Snider exercised was with their sufferance.

Even as they'd been meeting Carver in this very room, his advance teams had been silently moving in, sealing off the town ready for the arrival of the main forces the following morning. Mecklen was now under a Foundation blanket, snuffing out its former freedom.

Next to Snider sat Emilio Espinoza, the councilor who'd invited the Foundation in. The man looked wretched, seeming to shrink as Hannah and the others entered. It had only taken a few days for his folly to be revealed.

"Mayor Snider," Carver said, nodding to each of the newcomers, "Councilors Myers and Beale. We are now a quorum and can proceed."

Hannah slumped into the chair farthest from Carver and rubbed her eyes.

"I hope you're not unwell, Councilor," Carver said, turning his dark eyes on her.

"Why would I be?" Hannah snapped back. "Now we're in the loving embrace of the Foundation?"

Carver nodded, either missing the sarcasm or choosing to ignore it. "Indeed. You can all sleep soundly in your beds knowing that the streets are safe. Now, we will begin with Mr. Branch's report."

Branch emerged from the corner where he'd hidden like a chameleon. He consulted a clipboard, then, keeping his eyes fixed on Carver, said, "The city is secure, Representative. No fatalities or injuries to our people, but nine injuries sustained by locals. Twenty-two have been held for interrogation, five on charges of resisting Foundationers."

Ida let out a hiss of disbelief. "Twenty-two? So much for coming in peace."

"We have brought peace, Councilor," Carver said. "But, as I explained, we must be sure that the supplies we donate to the city won't be used to feed insurrectionists."

Hannah jabbed a finger at Carver. "How can someone be an insurrectionist in their own home?"

Sighing, Carver leaned back and directed his attention to Mayor Snider. "Must we explain our position to Councilor Myers, again?"

Snider shook his head. "No, Representative, please continue."

"What have your interrogations revealed, Branch?"

The weather-worn man ran his pencil down the clipboard. He sighed as if he were bored or exhausted. "Eight are Muslim, Representative, three are Hindu and all refuse to convert to the true faith. The others are accused of less serious crimes and, we're confident, can be brought into the brotherhood, except for Larry and Antoinette Craft."

Ida groaned. "Oh, for the love of God."

The room echoed to the sound of Carver's fist slamming down. "Do not take the Lord's name in vain, Councilor! This is your final warning," he said, before looking up at Branch, and calming down theatrically. "What of these people?"

"They claim to be atheists, Representative."

Carver's mouth hung open. "Impossible."

"We have attempted all our usual methods of persuasion and they refuse to recant."

"You understand our position on this matter, Branch?"

Again, Branch sighed. The man gave every impression of not wanting to be there. "I am not a cleric, but yes, I understand enough to carry out my function. There are no atheists, just deniers of the truth."

"Indeed. Any fool can see that our universe was created by an intelligent mind. They simply wish to deny it so that they may sin."

Hannah shifted in her chair, wondering what she would do if she were required to profess faith in the divine to save her life, let alone to align herself with the malicious doctrine of the Foundation.

She knew Larry and Tony Craft. Both retired, she'd spent pleasant time in their company reminiscing about the world before the fall. They were Humanists — a label that applied as well as any to Hannah herself. But, in these latter days, if you said you didn't believe in God, then the questioner rarely thought to ask what you *did* believe in. They rarely cared.

Hannah could quite believe that the Crafts would openly acknowledge their atheism, which put them at the head of the line for a one-way trip to hell, with the Muslims and Hindus just behind them on the down escalator.

"A pity," Carver said, steepling his fingers as if to demonstrate genuine concern. "I had hoped that the errors the people of Frederick's Town made would not be repeated here. I suppose the question for this council is to decide what to do with them."

Mitch Snider's face tightened. "What do you suggest? They haven't broken any civil laws."

"They have broken Foundation laws. Do you wish for us to deal with them?"

Hannah had to intervene. "No. I'll speak to them. Get them to sign on."

Leaning forward, Carver tapped the table with his pointer finger. "Sign on? This is a solemn matter, Doctor Myers. But we are not unreasonable. All they have to do is consent to be educated. *Then* they will take the oath."

"Uh huh," Ida said, "and what happens if they won't swear allegiance to the Foundation?"

Carver's dark, lidded eyes, turned in her direction. "If they refuse to acknowledge the many proofs we will offer them, then they will burn."

Silence hung in the room while Hannah held the gaze of each of the other councilors in turn, ending with Espinoza, who quickly looked away.

"And the Muslims?"

"They will also need re-education, as will any Christians who refuse to adopt our doctrinal principles."

"I thought you said you wanted to avoid any burnings?"

Carver shrugged. "That depends entirely on the citizens of Mecklen. And *that*, my dear councilors, depends on you, the figures of authority. Now, shall we return to more pleasant matters? Such as planning for the arrival of the supplies?"

***

"IF YOU'RE SO CLEVER, Hannah, why don't you tell me what the answer is? If we don't go along with what Carver wants, we're condemning dozens, maybe hundreds, to death. Do you think we can run the Foundation out of town?" Mitch Snider said.

"Of course not," Hannah said. They'd returned to her home, and she'd thoroughly checked it for any signs that Bobby might have been here in the meantime. Or, indeed, any Foundation spies.

They'd certainly been followed, and one of Branch's agents would be watching and hoping to catch their conversation, so they talked about the coming supplies and, in pauses, whispered privately. The problem was that Hannah was so furious about their situation that she was having trouble keeping the volume down.

"The thing is, Mitch, you're the mayor. You can decide whether to be a puppet, a collaborator like the ones appointed by the Germans in the Second World War, or whether you resist. Frankly, there's not much hope either way."

Mitch Snider gripped his head in his hands as if he could squeeze an idea out with enough effort. "I wish I'd never run for office. Mom said it'd end in tears."

"You know what they say about what comes with great power?"

Snider scowled, then in a louder voice, he said, "So we're agreed that the Ramos farm silo will be the central store, and we'll then send it to local distribution points? *Have you spoken to the Crafts?*"

"Yes, sounds like a plan. It'll be good to have enough to keep everyone through the winter. *Yes. They've been released for now, but they say they won't budge.*"

Snider sighed. "What about the local volunteer force? They know Carver will have them burned alive? *Can't they just pretend like the rest of us?*"

"Ida's getting a list together. They've all got to be vetted by the Foundation, obviously. *It's called having principles, Mitch.*"

"Of course, we only want trustworthy people handling food distribution. *I have principles, but I wouldn't go to the pyre rather than cross my fingers while I make the oath.*"

Hannah rolled her eyes. "Indeed. She should have the list within a couple of days. *I'm working on them. Then I'll go see the others.*"

Mitch Snider got to his feet, sending the kitchen chair scraping across the wooden surface. He leaned in close. "*You'll have to be amazingly creative to persuade them all. Jeez, Hannah, I can't have people in Mecklen going to the pyre.*" His face fell. "*I just don't know what to do. It's like a living nightmare.*"

"See you, Mr. Mayor. *I know. And it's only going to get worse.*"

Chapter 3

THE BARN

THEY PICKED THEIR WAY down the slope toward the column of smoke rising into the air before merging into the gray of the clouds.

Mercifully, the rain had stopped, but Reuben was hardly daring to look down at the boy in case he'd died. Asha hadn't moved for hours, just a dead weight in the former exciser's arms as he drove Lucifer on, Skeeter leading Blossom.

Skeeter had spotted the smoke first, at a point where Reuben was seriously considering plunging into the nearest wood and building a shelter to light a fire under, and damn the risk.

They'd been skirting to the north of Livingstone, AB, following what remained of I-20, now shrunken to a single-track road, the rest of the highway only recognizable as a shallow, flat depression in the ground. The steel barriers had been stripped away long ago and it wouldn't be many more years before this became nothing more than a grassy track in the Alabama wilderness.

"Look, boss!" Skeeter said, pointing ahead. He'd spurred his horse in front, pulling Blossom along behind him.

Reuben saw it as the building came into view behind a small stand of trees. From here, it looked like
a barn. With any luck, it was remote enough that
whoever ran the farm didn't visit it often, and they'd
be able to warm and feed the boy and get away
before they were even noticed. He didn't like relying
on luck, but they had no choice. Stop now, or Asha
would die.

"Slow down!" he called out as Skeeter accelerated
away into the open.

The younger man checked his horse and drew his
revolver, scanning the margins of the field. "Sorry,
boss. You're right. I don't see no one, though."

Reuben came alongside him as Blossom raised her
head to sniff at Asha's legs. Don't let him be dead,
Bane said to himself. Not after all this. He kicked
Lucifer on toward the building wondering why he
cared so much. Maybe this pain was the price of
caring enough to do the right thing.

The building was, indeed, a barn. It looked in
good repair, though the moss on the edges of the
thatched roof showed its age. As long as it was wa-
ter-tight, it'd do.

"Take him," Reuben said, sliding Asha down to
Skeeter, who had dismounted and was waiting for
orders.

Reuben watched as the young man lifted the
boy into arms so thin, they looked as though they
shouldn't be able to support him. Asha groaned and
Bane felt a wave of relief, and then turned on his
heels and drew his 1911.

He made his way warily toward the barn, Skeeter
following a few yards back, the reins of the horses
fixed to his belt. Reuben listened for any animal
sounds, but the barn was silent. He reached the

door, finding it padlocked, then settled down to pick the lock.

Around him, the woods were full of bird chatter and, despite his fear for Asha, he smiled as he forced his mind to relax. Hard to pick a lock with shaking hands. And as he did so, he became aware of the forest. He remembered the dead silence that had greeted him and his fellow survivors when they'd emerged from two weeks of hiding underground thirty-five years ago. The silence remained for a long time, the sounds of nature only returning slowly over the decades.

But he knew that the richness of the old world had disappeared. Where he would have heard a cacophony of species all competing with each other, now it was more of a monotone. He missed the hooting of owls and the wailing of kites, sounds of death that would never be heard again in all likelihood. The new world was one of excess — a small number of species occupying every available niche whether adapted for it or not. Bats flew in the daytime, dogs bred without control to form a nondescript admixture of experimental evolution, and rats grew huge in the sewers of the remaining cities. Mutated wolves, bears and mountain lions haunted the wild, especially in the west, and lurked on the dead margins of the old cities. Descendants of wise females who'd sheltered from the apocalypse in caves they'd given rise to clever hunters that threatened the countryside.

The lock fell apart and he pulled the bolt back, opening the barn door into the darkness beyond. He could instantly tell that there was nothing alive in here, but he swept the interior nonetheless as his eyes adjusted to the gloom. He held back a sneeze as his boots stirred dust into the air.

Various agricultural tools lay around the barn, some of them adapted from the old world, some repaired so many times they'd finally given up the ghost. Above, a mezzanine held several bails of dusty hay, and Reuben directed Skeeter to lay the boy down on a bed of straw on the timbered floor.

He kneeled beside Asha and ran his hand across the cold forehead. Well, he was alive, for now.

"Shall I make a fire, Boss?"

Reuben sighed, looking around at the dry, straw-strewn floor. "See if you can make a hearth while I get some ventilation in here. Strike a flame now and the whole place would go up with us inside."

He climbed to the mezzanine and opened the shutters, taking a deep breath as a cool breeze flowed in, clearing the air. From here, he could see a narrow band of grass that separated the barn from the line of trees beyond. A small flock of sheep nibbled at the edges, and he guessed the farmhouse must be in that direction, though he saw no signs of movement. He closed the shutters on this side, then checked on Skeeter who'd made a hearth out of loose bricks.

"I'm going to scout around," he said. "Check whether there's anything here we can eat, will you?"

He left Skeeter searching the corners of the barn and snuck out the door, making his way along the outer wall and peering around the corner. Lambs skittered playfully between the ewes, seemingly without a care in the world. He thought about the boy lying inside the barn, silently drew his knife and waited for the sheep to come closer.

REUBEN'S MOUTH WATERED AS he sat beside the camp-ing cauldron on its tripod and stirred. Skeeter had wanted to roast the lamb, but that would have sent up an aroma that would spread for miles around, so Reuben had instructed him to chop it into chunks while he looked for any herbs or weeds to go with it. He'd almost laughed out loud with delight when he found some apple-mint that was taking over a rotting section of brick wall, and it was this that he could smell now.

He'd also found water in a small stream that ran down the wooded slope. This place would have been perfect to lay up for a few days if it had been a little more remote, but the farmhouse turned out to be less than a mile away. He didn't think people came to the barn very often, but they'd have to keep watch. Once they'd eaten.

When the stew was ready, Reuben propped Asha up and woke him. The boy's eyes flicked open, and, for a moment, he looked into Bane's scarred face confused and frightened, then his expression set-tled.

"I ... I thought I was ..."

"In heaven?"

Skeeter howled with laughter before slapping his hand over his mouth. "And then you saw the boss's face and knew it couldn't be so. Did you think you'd gone to the other place?"

Asha didn't react, but focused on the bowl on an upturned barrel beside him.

"You have to eat," Reuben said.

"Don't … want …"

"No choice, Asha. Stay awake!" He shook the boy until his eyes opened again, then lifted the spoon to Asha's mouth even as his own stomach turned somersaults. "Here, sip it."

Reluctantly, Asha's lips parted, and he tasted the hot stew before Reuben offered up a chunk of meat. This was an exquisite torture for a starving man, but he smiled as the boy chewed and swallowed, his enthusiasm growing.

Skeeter reached over and felt Asha's forehead. "He's still cold."

"Uh-huh. He needs more than food. He needs rest and warmth, but first he must refuel his body so it can fight whatever's ailing him."

"You reckon we might get it, too?"

"Maybe, but we're both older, tougher and uglier than him, so we can endure it."

Skeeter chuckled. "Ain't that the truth, Boss. I feel as tired as death, but I reckon that's more cos I'm so hungry my stomach thinks my throat's been cut."

"You'll get your turn soon enough."

Reuben continued to feed Asha as if he were nursing an infant, listening to the sounds of the birds outside and the sheep bleating. They'd been scattered when he'd seized the lamb, but had obviously returned. They really were the most stupid of animals.

"Anyone moves," a woman's voice shouted into the barn, "and I'll fill him full of buckshot and burn the barn down."

Chapter 4

THE MARK

"WATCH THEM, LEO," THE woman said to the young boy who followed her into the barn. She carried an ancient double-barreled shotgun and was obviously comfortable with the weapon.

Reuben's arm still cradled Asha and he couldn't possibly reach his weapon even if he felt inclined to.

She wore a stained woolen plaid skirt and a white shirt beneath an apron, and she jabbed the gun at Reuben. "You son of a bitch! Poaching one of my lambs."

"I'm sorry, ma'am," he said, keeping half an eye on the barrel that vibrated with rage. "We were in desperate need. I can pay. I have silver."

"I don't take silver from brigands."

"I am no brigand, ma'am."

Her eyes rose to his face as he tilted his head back. He saw the shock there as she took in his scars, but she masked it well. "Well, we got laws in these lands, God knows we pay a high enough price for them. Don't expect mercy from the sheriff, but you shouldn't have stolen from me. We need the meat and the wool."

"As I said, I'll pay. If not with silver, then by sweat. I am not particularly skilled in any craft, but I am not afraid of hard work. Your husband will know what to set me to."

The woman's face froze for a moment, then she said to the boy behind her, "Take their weapons, then go fetch your father."

The boy went to argue, but she shushed him, and he padded over to where Reuben sat.

"What's wrong with him?" she asked, as if she'd only just noticed Asha.

"He got sick during our journey. That's why we sheltered here. He's near starving, so I killed one of your animals and I'm genuinely sorry. But I'm responsible for him. He won't die on my account if I can help it. My name is Reuben Bane, and these are my friends, Skeeter and Asha. Please don't judge us too quickly."

The shotgun barrel twitched as she let out a mirthless chuckle. "Not for me to do. We've got men paid to do the judging, and I'll leave it to them. They keep enough in taxes, they might as well earn it."

"Even if it means the boy suffers?"

Her eyes narrowed, but he detected sympathy. She was a woman of unremarkable appearance, except for eyes that seemed to look inside him and read his mind. A woman used to the harsh realities of the post-apocalyptic world she'd been born into.

At that moment, Reuben heard movement behind him and turned to find Skeeter with his arms around the young boy's waist. "I got you. Now, how's about you put that gun down, ma'am, before any of us gets hurt."

"Let him go!" the woman cried out, "or so help me, God, I'll put a bullet in your friend's brain."

Reuben remained motionless, but tried to reassure Skeeter. "Let the boy go."

"But boss, she's gonna turn us into the law! Sure as eggs, they'll judge us for poachers and string us up."

"I have faith that this lady will listen to what we have to say fairly, and then we will allow her to make the choice. She is right enough; we have trespassed, and stolen from her. Go ahead, let him go."

Skeeter looked doubtful, but finally opened his arms and the boy ran back to his mother as Reuben turned to her. "We are in your hands, ma'am. We will not resist. All I ask is you listen."

She gripped the boy against her hip, then looked first at Skeeter, then Reuben, then Asha, who hadn't stirred.

"That little one looks close to the end," she said, her tone gentler. "Okay, I think I can trust you, but throw your weapons over there and Leo will cover me." She handed the shotgun to the boy. "And don't you worry, he knows how to use it right enough."

"I don't doubt it Mrs..."

"Drew."

"Mrs. Drew. May I ask where your husband is?"

Her shoulders sagged as she kneeled to examine Asha. "He's been dead these two years. There's just me, Leo here and Mike. He's my husband's father."

"Do you wish to call him?"

"This is my farm, Mr. Bane, I don't need help from any man."

"I don't doubt it, lady. Now, will you hear our story?"

"I'm no lady. And you won't try to stop me calling the sheriff if I have a mind to?"

"That will always be your prerogative for as long as we remain on your property."

She nodded. "Then speak, Mr. Bane. And don't even think about telling a lie."

ASHA LAY IN THE bed, breathing gently as Mrs. Drew looked over him. "He's pretty sick. I reckon you'll be staying here for a few days."

"I can't thank you enough, ma'am," Reuben said. They'd brought Asha to the farmhouse and installed him in Leo's bedroom despite protests from the boy and his grandfather. The old man was confined to an antique wheelchair with flat tires, however, and it was obvious who was mistress here.

"You'll thank me by working, as you agreed."

"I will."

"And my name's Angelina, but everyone calls me Angel."

He couldn't help raising his eyebrows.

She laughed. "Yea, it's either ironic or wishful thinking. My poor husband, Rene, always said he liked a strong woman, and I guess he got what he wished for and more than he asked for."

"How did he die? Do you mind me asking?"

She smoothed the blankets and tucked them under Asha's arms. "He was killed by Simmons' men. Claimed he'd gone to draw his weapon, but Noel would never do that."

"I'm sorry, Angel. But why did they want him dead?"

She shrugged. "They want this land, but they want to do it legal. Or, at least, to look legal. I reckon Simmons actually believes he's a good man, but this farm once belonged to his family, and it's got the best grazing and timber in the valley. He wants it back. Figured I wouldn't be able to cope on my own, so he'd be able to step in and buy it from me when I gave in."

"He obviously doesn't know you."

"Well, he does now, for sure," she said, smiling, then she straightened up and moved closer to him. "But truth is, I can't manage on my own and with a young boy as my only help. Poor Mike, it cuts him to the bone that he can't help more, but that's the fact of it. There's not much he can do."

Reuben gestured at the sleeping boy. "You think he'll make it?"

"I'm an optimist, but now, how about you?"

She moved toward him, and he reflexively stepped back in surprise.

"What about me?"

"Your arm." Reaching out, she took his left hand and lifted it, so the sleeve of his shirt slipped past the bandage. Reuben resisted for a moment, but then relaxed and let her examine it.

He watched her face as she unwrapped the binding.

"How in heaven did you do this?"

He'd thought about a plausible excuse during the long hours of riding over the previous days. He'd fallen against a rusting car. He'd fought with bandits, but taken a glancing cut to his arm. He'd done it by misusing a scythe. But he didn't have a chance to select the least worst of them, because she spoke first.

"This was an exciser's mark," she whispered, looking up at him in confusion and fear. "I've only been up close with an exciser once, when Leo was accused by a vindictive neighbor, but it was just here. I ... I don't understand."

Reuben sighed. He hadn't been touched with such gentleness since beginning his journey east months ago. "Before I answer, tell me this. Will you care for my friends, especially the boy? They are not part of this."

"I will. Now, speak the truth."

"I *was* an exciser, for many years. But I repented and have sought to repay the evil I did in some small way."

"That's why you are caring for the boy? He's a deviant?"

Nodding, Reuben looked directly into her eyes. The dogma about those with any kind of difference was hammered into people from birth, and many couldn't see past it. "He has skin between his toes, that's all. Do you withdraw your promise to look after him?"

"Carry on with your account, first."

"The Foundation has hunted me for many months. Finally, their agents caught up with me. This was just the first of many intended torments on my way to New Boston."

She gasped, her face flushing as she jabbed a finger at him. "Don't you see what you've done? I make you welcome, and you would bring the Foundation to my door? They'll accuse me of hiding a fugitive and kill us all!"

"My pursuers are no longer a problem."

"Why?"

"They are dead."

"You killed them?"

Reuben nodded. In truth, Asha had killed the apprentice, but she didn't need to know that.

"So, you're still a murderer? I don't want a killer under my roof."

An overwhelming darkness swept over him as he looked at this woman. Life certainly had been simpler when he hadn't been burdened with the ability to see the world out of the eyes of others. Empathy was an inconvenience. "I will depart tomorrow. May I sleep in the barn tonight?"

"What about your other friend?"

"Skeeter? He has a good soul and might be useful here. He's a willing lad and will follow your instructions."

"I'll think about it."

He turned to go. "I will say this, ma'am. I am no threat to you, but I do seem to attract misfortune and violence even though I no longer seek it."

"What would you do, in my shoes?"

He smiled, sadly. "I think, exactly what you are doing. You can't see inside my heart, so you must decide on the evidence you have. I deserve no better from you."

Reuben felt her eyes on him as he left the room, picked up his pack and walked back to the barn as night fell.

Chapter 5

ZAK

HE COULDN'T BREATHE. ALL he could hear was the laughter of his opponent, all he could feel was the pain in his ribs. Forcing his diaphragm to relax, Zak drew air into his aching lungs and used the wall he'd collided with to get to his feet.

A few yards away, Kurt maintained the prescribed stance, though he was struggling to contain his amusement. Only the presence of Master Sergeant Barber kept his discipline in place.

Zak wanted nothing more than to curl up in a ball and sleep, but there was no escape. He'd been training with Barber for a week now, and the pain would only end when the Master Sergeant released him, or he succumbed to an ill-directed blow from one of this fellow trainees.

He'd been scared enough when Father Ruiz had said he'd be training with Barber, but his terror had increased tenfold when he realized he was only going to be one amongst many. And the others had already spent weeks under the sergeant's tutelage, and all were older and bigger than him.

To begin with, he'd found strength in the prospect of becoming protector to the beautiful Eve, but soon enough he'd replaced that with focusing on surviving the day and hoping that, at some point, the pain would end one way or another.

He held up his sword. It was a training weapon, with no stabbing point and a blunt edge, but it could be used as a pretty effective club if he didn't defend himself effectively.

Kurt smiled and leaped forward, Zak only just managing to sidestep, so the sword stroke hit the brick wall of the basement they used for training, and the watching students winced as one.

As Kurt yelled, his sword limp in his hand, Zak stepped back, waiting for his opponent to indicate he was ready.

And he was still waiting when, with the speed of a diving hawk, Kurt kicked out, catching Zak in the chest and propelling him across the floor to tumble in the dust.

Kurt was on him in a moment, pressing the blunt end of his weapon to Zak's throat.

"I yield," Zak croaked.

The sword remained there for a moment, before being withdrawn, and he was left on the floor looking up as Kurt took the congratulations of his fellows.

The heavy-set face of Barber loomed above Zak. "You are a fool. You had your chance and missed it. Do not step back, do not give quarter. He took advantage and, if this was real life, your blood would be soaking into the dust."

"Sorry, master," Zak said, groaning as he got to his feet.

"You will clean the arena," Barber said without looking at him.

"But master. It's not my turn. And I need to see the sawbone."

Barber scowled. "You'll see the medic when your work is done. You're precious little use as a fighter, so you might as well do what you're good at. Women's work. Cleaning."

Anger flared in Zak's chest, but he'd learned not to strike back instinctively. The quickest route to rest and healing was to do as the sergeant said.

The man regarded him for a moment and then nodded. "Well done, boy. You held your temper back, and most wouldn't have even noticed how close you came to losing your shit. I did, though."

Despite the pain, Zak blushed. "Thank you, master."

"But that was the most pathetic fighting performance I've seen since I walked in on two maids fighting in the kitchen. You've got to catch up, boy or, for your sake and Father Ruiz's, I'll have to send you back."

Panic flooded Zak's stomach. "No, please, master!"

Quite apart from the humiliation, the chances of Ruiz keeping on a servant who'd been rejected by the master sergeant were remote. It wasn't fair. But then, nothing was.

Barber didn't say a word, he simply turned on his heels and walked away, leaving Zak alone in the dark basement.

"YOU OKAY, SQUIRT? DID I hurt you bad?"

Zak cursed himself for wincing as he pulled on his linen shirt before heading up to serve Father Ruiz. It underlined how miserable his existence with Barber was that Zak looked forward with relief to emptying the priest's chamber pot.

"Get lost, Kurt."

The young man smirked, though Zak noticed the cut on his opponent's cheekbone where one of his strokes had gotten past Kurt's defenses.

"You goin' upstairs to wipe your master's butt? Wanna do mine first?"

Zak snapped. He jumped up, fists balled and caught Kurt with a vicious uppercut that left him staggering away backwards and falling over a bed to end up in a pile on the floorboards.

Zak should have left him there and hurried upstairs to serve his master, but he was a kind-hearted soul and, not for the first or last time, that now betrayed him.

As he climbed on the bed and looked over the edge to see if he'd knocked his opponent out, Kurt exploded, fist flying upwards to connect with Zak's jaw. Then he was on top of Zak, face contorted with ungovernable rage, fingers wrapping around Zak's throat, sucking the life out of him.

Kicking out desperately, Zak tried to get him off, tried to call out for help, but then darkness spread from the edge of his sight inward, and he felt himself slipping away even as he grasped at the hands that were throttling him.

Then Kurt was gone and over him stood the big figure of Master Sergeant Barber.

He had hold of Kurt by the back of his neck and was holding him up effortlessly even as he struggled.

Barber looked directly at Zak, eyes glowing with barely contained fury. "Get out of here."

"I'm ... I'm sorry, M—"

"Go!"

It was the first time he'd ever seen Master Sergeant Barber lose his temper and that, more than anything else, snapped him out of it and he turned for the door, desperately trying to draw air into his lungs and grabbing at his bruised throat.

And as he went, he heard Kurt call out. "I'm gonna kill you. Hear me? I'm gonna —"

Zak heard what sounded like a body hitting the floor, but he didn't turn around, he merely ran for it.

"WHAT IN THE NAME of the Holy Father is the meaning of this?" Father Ruiz roared as Zak opened the door to the priest's chamber, and stood, panting in front of his master.

He'd prayed that Ruiz would still be asleep when he arrived, as he often was, but since meeting his young prospective bride, Eve, he'd sworn off drink and the prostitutes who normally shared his bed. This had already had the unfortunate affect, from Zak's perspective, of making him more energetic and more likely to wake early.

"I'm sorry, Father," he said, straightening the collar of his shirt.

Ruiz, who'd been sitting on the side of his bed in his night-clothes, got to his feet and approached the boy. "Your throat is bruised. Is Master Sergeant Barber teaching his trainees how to throttle their enemies? It is an unseemly and inefficient method of despatch, I would think."

That was certainly true, Zak thought. Strangulation was one of the Foundation's favorite methods of execution, reserved generally for those who spoke against the religion.

"No, Father, he doesn't teach that."

Zak could see Ruiz's curiosity expiring. He was a man whose main interest was himself, and the problems of his servant didn't concern him much, unless they impacted him.

Ruiz dismissed the matter with a huff, and turned around for Zak to help remove his nightshirt.

The boy had seen his hairy, wart encrusted back often enough to be immune to the disgust he'd felt the first time he'd had to do this. He simply took the garment — fine linen that was only good for a dozen washes — and handed Ruiz the white collarless shirt that had been left on the dresser the previous night.

"How do you progress with the Master Sergeant?" Ruiz said.

"It's not for me to say, Father. I try my best."

Ruiz swung around, "Try? You must do more than try! You must succeed!"

"I'm sorry, Father."

"Do I have to remind you how vital it is that Eve has protection I can trust?"

"No, Father. I will succeed, I promise."

Ruiz's face softened. At first, Zak had simply been delighted to get a chance to learn fighting skills, but the mystery of why Ruiz was so insistent on its importance had tugged at his mind. Why did it matter *so* much that Eve had protection? And if it *was* that vital, why not find someone who was already trained?

"You must, my boy. You must. Now, please attend to your duties, I have a busy day ahead."

Ruiz's smile made Zak feel like a particularly re-calcitrant puppy, but he returned a gentle reflection and hurried to find the chamber pot under the bed.

Chapter 6

STEW

"WHERE DO YOU THINK you're going?"

Reuben looked over Lucifer's back to see Angelina Drew striding toward him, the shotgun nestling in the crook of her arm.

He'd had little sleep, and had hoped to get away unnoticed soon after dawn.

"I am leaving," he said as she shooed away the flock of sheep who followed at her heels.

"So much for your fine words about repaying the debt with work."

Reuben sighed as he tightened the saddle. "Lady, you made it plain last night that you wished me to go. I am obliging."

She halted a few feet from Lucifer and stood with her hands on her hips. "Well, I've slept on it since then and, after all, you didn't sneak into the house and murder me in my sleep."

"I'm too tired to work out whether you are joking. Please, speak plainly."

Angelina let out a deep breath. "I spoke with Skeeter, and had some words with Asha."

"He's awake?"

She nodded. "In the small hours, for a time. I'm not sure he understands who you are, really, but he's told me what you've done to keep him alive when it would have been easier to abandon him. That says a lot about you."

"I'm pleased the boy is healing. But I don't understand myself any more than Asha does, though I know with certainty that you have nothing to fear from me."

"I get that," she said, seeming to relax a little. "I thought about it when I was sitting with Asha. You could have stayed an exciser and lived a life of luxury and respect, even if you didn't believe it any longer. But you turned your back on the Foundation and became a marked man. You'll never have peace, you know that don't you?"

He shrugged. "I will have peace when I have completed my tasks. What happens next is not my concern. My soul is too polluted by evil for me to have any hope that I can redeem myself. I am destined for hell, Angel. Perhaps it would be better for you if I were to ride on now, as I intended."

"That boy needs you. Sooner or later, he will be examined, and they'll find his ... deviance. Seems to me, the safest place he can be is beside a former exciser."

Reuben shook his head, then ran his hands down the back of Lucifer's neck, scratching his mane. "Likely enough he'll be caught either way, but at least if he stays here, he'll be comfortable for a while."

"And what will the excisers do when they realize I've sheltered a mutant?"

He groaned. "You are right, of course. It is better for you if Asha comes with me."

"You make me sound like a selfish, frightened old woman."

"You are none of those things, Angel. You have your son and father-in-law to think about."

She looked at him for a moment, as if giving time for her intuition to raise its hand before she decided. Angelina Drew had a square face with a robust jawline and blue eyes bordered by crows-feet that deepened as she thought. She was the kind of woman most men would walk past. The lucky one would see her for what she was.

"What are you thinking?" he asked.

She started as if snapped out of contemplation, and her hand went to the line of her chin. "My heart says I can trust you. I think if you were here to do me harm, you'd, I don't know, look better, but my gut would warn me. You're the other way round."

"I feel foul but look fair, you mean?" Reuben said, smiling and making a mental note to restart *The Fellowship of the Ring* on his ebook reader that night.

"Exactly, no offence meant."

"None taken, lady. To quote Aragorn, I fear my looks are against me."

She returned his smile, and it was as if the spell were broken. "We'll call that agreed then. I'll feed you, house you and care for your friend, and you'll do some work on the farm and promise not to kill me in my sleep."

"That is an easy promise to make," he said, saddened that the jest clearly masked lingering discomfort. He would give all he had to simply be trusted, but he followed her back toward the house, leading Lucifer and wondering whether he could keep his promise. Of course, he wouldn't hurt her directly, but the people around him had a habit of coming to harm whether he willed it or not.

REUBEN SAT ON THE silo roof, legs astride the ridge, and smoothed the mortar along the seam of the ridge tile. After joining the Foundation, he'd done little manual work, until he'd moved to the small property in Illinois he'd purchased with his retirement silver. At that time, he'd been relieved to have left the organization, having shut away the darkness that had crept up on him over the years.

He'd met Marianna on a trip into the nearest market for supplies. Her father was a merchant, and he'd worked tirelessly to bring them together. There were few more respected positions in a community than the wife of an exciser, and Marianna had, in the end, acquiesced to her father's wishes. Reuben knew she'd fallen in love with him in the end, but he hadn't provided her with the security and status her father had sought. Because two years after they were married, she bore a daughter who had one extra finger on each hand.

"Boss!"

Reuben was snapped out of his memories by the voice of Skeeter from below.

"What is it?"

"Are you done up there?"

"Yes."

"Then Mrs. Drew said to say she's serving supper."

Reuben smiled and suddenly realized how hungry he was, the sensation blowing away the cloud that had gathered in his mind. Thinking was not good in large doses, he'd met his wife five years ago now on the day he'd renounced his position, though the Foundation didn't discover this for many months.

"My, you stink to high heaven," Angelina Drew said as Reuben and Skeeter walked into the kitchen and approached the large oak table. "You'll take a shower before sitting down to eat."

"You have a shower?" Reuben said, his hunger momentarily forgotten.

"We have, and there's even hot water."

Angelina laughed at his expression of disbelief. "You can thank Mike for that, he converted the furnace."

"Oh, it's alright. I'm old enough to remember a real shower. I don't miss much about the old world, but warm water's one thing I do. Put it into my place, and then did it again for Angel when she married my Noel."

Reuben strode across and shook the old man by the hand with such genuine joy that Mike couldn't resist smiling back with pride.

IT WAS A CLEANER and more fragrant Reuben Bane who returned to the table half an hour later. Angelina had left clothes for him to change into outside the bathroom, and he'd felt self-conscious as he pulled on the shirt of her dead husband. But boy was it good to be washed and to wear clean clothes.

Reuben had ordered Skeeter to wash first, and any discomfort Angel and Mike might have felt about them wearing Noel's clothes was broken when the young man emerged, looking like a child in dress up. He'd been forced to tie a knot in the belt to keep the jeans in place and he flushed as red as a strawberry as he sat at the table and Reuben left to clean up himself.

By the time he returned from one of the most blissful experiences of his life — one of many he'd taken for granted before the fall — the others had eaten, so he had the remainder of the vegetable stew to himself. As an avowed carnivore in the old world, he'd learned to accept a more varied diet that included little meat and just about any edible vegetable imaginable. His work as an exciser meant he'd been taught how to survive on his own in the wild, so he knew how to find food in almost any situation. He'd eaten Saguaro fruit in the western desert and dandelion leaves in the Michigan countryside. But that was just eating to survive. Mrs. Drew's stew was truly the food of angels.

Angelina disappeared with Leo and a small bowl to tend to Asha who was now sitting up in bed and, when she returned, Mike had poured Skeeter and Reuben a jug of beer and the three men were relaxing in the residual warmth of the stove.

An hour later, just as Reuben was drifting into a satiated half sleep, a bell sounded, and he jumped to his feet. "What was that?"

"That's the alarm, someone's coming," Mike said.

Angelina scowled and looked over at the kitchen clock. "That'll be Clem."

"Who's Clem?"

"He owns the next farm. His daddy's mighty close with Simmons."

"The same man who had your husband murdered?"

Her face went rigid. "I'll deal with him. You stay here and don't show yourself, d'you hear me? He mustn't know you're here."

Reuben nodded, his convivial mood having vanished in seconds, and watched as she shut the kitchen door behind her.

"He wants to court her," Mike said, looking up at Reuben.

"Why?" Bane said, without thinking. "I mean, she's a fine woman, but ..."

"There are younger women in Livingstone, but they don't own a hundred acres of prime planting and grazing land. If you go around to the window there, you'll be able to hear what's said, but don't you interfere, or she'll never trust you again."

Reuben nodded and thanked the old man, then tiptoed over to the window and pressed his ear to the wall.

He could hear a man's voice, though he spoke quietly, as if afraid of being overheard. "You gotta understand, Angel, this is the only way you keep your land."

"You don't get to call me Angel, Clem Bolger, and if you get your way, it won't be *my* land anymore, will it? It'll be yours."

There was a pause. "I'm sorry you see it like that, Mrs. Drew, but my daddy is the only protection you're gonna get from Gabe Simmons getting his hands on this place."

"He doesn't have any right; he can't just steal land from folks!"

"Well, it'll be all legal, like. But it'll happen, unless ..."

There was the sound of a double-barreled shotgun being snapped shut. "Now you listen here, you son of a bitch, if you're not off my property by the time I count to ten, you won't be qualified to marry nobody. D'you hear me! Get out of here!"

The conversation devolved into shouted words he couldn't separate but, finally, Bolger got the message and withdrew.

"I'll be back in a few days, Mrs. Drew, to get your final answer."

"You've had my answer!"

"Maybe I have, maybe you'll see things different come Friday."

And the door slammed behind him.

Chapter 7

RAFIQ

HANNAH SAT AT THE modest kitchen table waiting for her tea to be poured.

"What have you come to tell us, Councilor? That we must bend the knee to your religion?"

Hannah couldn't help a grim chuckle escaping. "The Foundation isn't my religion, Mr. Rafiq," she said. "Thank you. Smells delicious." As she waited for Mrs. Rafiq to sit, she raised her cup and breathed in through her nose. "Smells like orange pekoe, or, at least how I remember it."

The young woman smiled. She was striking, with orange hair and blue eyes, in contrast to her husband's light brown. In fact, if a stranger had entered the room now, they'd have automatically believed Hannah to be Rafiq's wife since they were much more alike.

There was a story to be told here. Even thirty-five years after the fall, people of religion tended to marry other members of their particular faith. But that story would have to wait.

"I was lucky. Amir had some seeds."

"They came from my family in Sri Lanka a few years before the fall," Amir Rafiq said, his face transformed by a wide smile. "I was a child, but I kept the seeds through everything that happened. And then I met Sarah, and when we came to make our home here, she decided to see if they would grow."

She took his hand. "We've got three bushes in the back yard, and that's enough for us and to have a little spare. It's a taste of home for Amir. But look, this isn't what you came here to talk about, is it, Councilor?"

"I wish it was," Hannah said, her mood, which had lifted briefly, now darkened again. She lowered her voice. "Would one of you mind taking a look outside? See if anyone might be able to overhear?"

Amir Rafiq nodded and went to the window. It looked to Hannah as though he struggled to get to his feet. Maybe the couple of days spent in detention had exhausted him.

The Rafiqs lived in a townhouse that was, effectively, part of the defensive wall protecting the center of the city, and looked outward. "I see nothing unusual, but perhaps we should close the window."

"Mr. and Mrs. Rafiq," Hannah said as Amir returned to his chair at the table. "You know the situation. For better or worse, we allowed the Foundation into Mecklen, and we can't put the genie back in its bottle. So, we each have to decide what we do about it."

Sarah Rafiq shrugged. "What are our options? Submit or we'll be killed as heretics?"

"Well, it's true that there's no gray area with the Foundation, except that if you consent to attend their classes, you'll buy some time."

"Time for what? They're not going anywhere."

Hannah rubbed her temples. "I don't know. Time to think, maybe? I can't believe the only options are to bend the knee or die."

"It has happened many times in history," Amir said.

"Look, all I ask is that you stall for time by attending the classes. They're not going to convert you, after all, are they?"

Sarah shook her head. "For Amir, his religion is part of who he is."

"And for you?"

"My faith is unshakeable. What's the point in living a lie?"

"It's the living part that's the point."

The chair under Sarah creaked as she leaned back. "I don't know why you care so much. I can't have children."

Hannah's jaw dropped. "What's that got to do with anything?"

"You're the population professor, aren't you? You think we're going to die out. Well, whether I'm alive or not, I won't be playing any part in saving humanity."

"Let me ask you this, Sarah," Hannah said, biting down on her rising rage, "how many kids do you think I have?"

Uncertainty clouded Sarah Rafiq's pretty face, but Hannah beat her to the punch.

"That's right, none living, zero. Do I regret that? Absolutely I do. Does that mean I don't have value? Of course not. A woman's value as a human being isn't defined by how many children she has, any more than a man with a low sperm count."

"But ..."

"Yes, I've been studying population dynamics for the best part of twenty years, and, yes, looking at the raw numbers our birth rate is too low, but having more babies isn't the solution on its own. If we're going to be all Darwinian about this, children have to survive long enough to have children themselves, and that's a matter for the whole of society."

Amir nodded, looking across at his wife. "I think we both understand this, Doctor. Forgive my wife, it is a ... difficult matter."

Hannah's anger dissipated like smoke on the breeze. "I get it, I really do. Please don't sacrifice yourselves unnecessarily."

"Standing by our beliefs isn't unnecessary," Amir said. "But we hear you. We will talk about it and, perhaps, agree to undertake the Foundation classes. But please don't press us. This whole thing has exhausted us both. It's hard to be interrogated in your hometown simply for being who you've always been.

"In the meantime, we put our trust in you to find a solution because we will not take an oath that would betray our beliefs. To do so would be to sacrifice all we believe in this life and suffer an eternity of regret and punishment."

HANNAH HAD BARELY REACHED street level when the siren went off. Instinctively, she looked at the strip of cloth on her jacket sleeve, seeing no sign of a glow even when she shielded it. But she'd been indoors for an hour, so maybe it hadn't had time to register. People scattered, scurrying for cover, knowing as little as she did.

She lengthened her stride as she headed through the guarded alley into the inner circuit of Mecklen. Batting away the questions the guards fired at her as she went, she was almost running as she emerged into the daylight again.

City hall was like a kicked-over ants' nest, but almost everyone she saw running up and down the steps was Foundation.

Then an ancient diesel truck fired up and people began boarding it. It looked for all the world as if the Foundation was leaving town.

She saw Mitch Snider running down the steps two at a time.

"What the hell, Mitch? Is it an aurora?"

He was puffing as he reached the bottom and stood for a moment shaking his head and drawing breath into his lungs. "No."

"They're not leaving, are they?"

Snider straightened up, his face flushed red. "Yeah."

"What the f—?"

He made a motion as if he was washing an invisible window two-handed.

Before he could speak, Carver appeared. He went to walk past them, but Hannah grabbed his arm.

"What's going on?" Hannah said.

He twisted on her, in a mix of anger and fear. "Get your hands off me! You've gotten your wish, Doctor. We're leaving, for now. But we'll be back."

"I don't understand."

"It's the Crafts," Mitch managed.

Hannah felt her insides turn to ice. "What about them?"

Carver stabbed a finger at her. "They have brought the wrath of God upon us! I shouldn't have listened to you. If they'd perished in purifying flames, this would not have happened. The Lord is furious with us for suffering those who defy him to live. Once he has consumed the guilty in his righteous vengeance, then we will return."

He swung away and half-ran toward the waiting truck before climbing into the front seat.

Hannah gaped open-mouthed at Mitch.

"Plague," he said, "they've got the plague."

Chapter 8

Magic

REUBEN SAT ON THE garden bench, cradling a bottle of Mike's homebrew beer as he brooded. He'd had Angel on his mind ever since the unwelcome visit of the night before.

She'd refused point blank to discuss the matter that evening, and he'd spent the day finishing the repairs to the silo roof with Skeeter, but that hadn't stopped him turning the matter over and over. He saw what was happening, plain as anything. It was the power of money talking. That and the lack of protection for women outside of marriage.

The topic hadn't been broached over dinner, and he'd taken himself outside for fear that his mood might infect the others. Asha was recovering, but they would be here for a few more days and he wanted the atmosphere to return to how it had been before Clem had turned up.

"Son of a bitch," he said, before swigging on the bottle.

"Who?"

He spun around to see Angel approaching.

"I'm sorry," he said. "I didn't hear you. I apologize for my bad language. I'm not a cultured man."

She laughed at that and sat down beside him, the chair creaking under her. "Now, that's just nonsense. Most folks in these parts can barely read, but you've been an exciser, so you know your Bible at least. And I know what you've got in your pack."

His shock was so obvious, she patted his wrist. "I'm sorry, I saw it, I didn't touch it. It's right where it was when you left it this morning."

"It's okay. It's precious to me. Very precious."

"I've never seen one before. Seems like magic. Will you show me?"

He felt a surge of emotion for her in that moment. What was it? He'd been in love before, but this didn't feel quite like that. A wide grin spread across his face as he jumped up. "I'll go fetch it."

"It is magic," she said as she cradled the battered e-reader in her hands and examined it closely.

He grunted dismissively, though he was, in truth, delighted. Few enough people in this latter-day world valued reading. "You should have seen it when it was new. I just hope I can keep it going for a few years longer."

"How is it powered?"

He pointed at the screen, fingers running over the familiar scratches. "I have a small solar panel. In sunny weather, it'll charge fully in a day, and then it'll last a month or two."

"Uh-huh." She nodded. Even after thirty-five years, solar panels were relatively common. Solar technology was simple enough, it was the batteries it powered that broke down irreplaceably. "How many books have you got on here?"

"Three hundred and thirty-one."

Her jaw dropped open. "And you've read them all?"

"No. This wasn't my device, so it's someone else's collection. He or she had a penchant for French literature, so half of the library is lost to me. Fortunately, they also loved the classics, so I've got enough Dickens, Elliot, Tolkien and Steinbeck to last."

"How did you come across it?"

"It was soon after the first wave. You have to understand, we had no choice but to take what we could from the houses of the dead, like carrion crows. The place I found this had burned down but I saw it when I turned over the remains of a bed. The mattress had protected it. I couldn't stand to see it destroyed by rain or a careless boot. Even back then, I knew how precious working tech would be. So, I took it underground with me."

She put her hand on his arm, full of attention. "Tell me about that time. Mike said it was like being in hell."

"Where did he shelter?"

"An underground parking lot. He won't talk about it."

"I don't blame him. I was in an old mine: it had been a museum and we took farm animals with us. It was ... hard. I learned that it wasn't only nature we should be frightened of, it was other people. I guess that started me along the road to ..."

She withdrew her hand and moved apart from him a little. It was as if the warmth had been leached from the air. "To becoming an exciser?"

He nodded, missing her closeness. "I don't wish to speak of it."

"Okay," she responded, sitting back and looking out at the darkening garden. "I can't pretend it doesn't matter to me what you were, but I try to judge people by their actions now, not what they were a long time ago."

"You're a kind woman, Angel."

The hand returned to his forearm. "No, I really am not. I don't forgive easy, but I also don't bear grudges towards folks who haven't done me harm."

They sat silently for a few minutes, before Reuben asked the question that had been occupying his mind. "Tell me about Clem Bolger."

She made a groaning noise in her throat. "It's best you don't get too involved, Reuben. His father owns the next farm along. He's a close buddy of Simmons."

"You think he had anything to do with your husband's murder?"

He saw confirmation in her eyes, despite the non-committal shrug.

"Do you not wish for justice?"

"Justice is for those who can afford it."

"What of revenge?"

She sighed. "I don't have the luxury of that. I've got Leo and Mike to think of."

"If you say the word ..." Reuben began.

"No! I won't have blood spilled on my account. It would only bring more trouble, you understand? Promise me you'll leave Clem and his pa alone." She'd turned in her seat and was facing him, eyes searching his hard expression.

He sighed. "As you wish. I think, perhaps, the sooner we leave, the better."

REUBEN WAS IN THE bedroom talking to Asha when the first shots rang out. The boy was healing well, though he could do with another couple of days of rest that he wouldn't get.

He sprang up and ran to the window. In the darkening dusk he could see horses galloping down the slope from the direction of the highway. The same direction he and the others had come from five days before.

His first thought was that it was the posse from Jackson, and he ran down the stairs, pulling his Colt 1911 and taking his short sword from its place at the door before striding into the half-light. He could see flames bobbing up and down.

Angelina ran in from the kitchen, double barreled shotgun in her arms.

"Brigands," she said.

Reuben shook his head. "Brigands don't generally burn before they steal, and yet they're heading for the barn, aren't they?"

Before waiting for an answer, he ran to the small lean-to that functioned as a stable and climbed quickly onto Lucifer's back.

"I'm with you, boss," Skeeter shouted, as he threw his leg over the back of his gelding.

As he guided Lucifer into the open, he saw another animal emerge from behind the house. "Stay here, Mrs. Drew!" he called out.

Her curse was so foul and fluent it hit him like a magical blow, but he snapped out of it in time to kick Lucifer ahead and the big black gelding soon outpaced the other horses.

He jumped down when they reached the shelter of a small stand of trees.

Five, no six, riders circled the barn, torches raised high. It was as if they wanted to be sure they could be seen from the farmhouse.

He felt Angelina push past him on foot and tried to grab her, but was too late. She strode into the flickering light and yelled at the riders.

"You get your filthy hides off my land or, so help me God, I'll fill you full of holes."

The riders stopped and parted as one made his way to the front. All wore masks and had their wide-brimmed hats drawn low at the front so their faces couldn't be seen.

The leader raised his hand, and the others lowered their weapons. "You are alone, woman?"

"No! My husband is gathering the posse, you'd better get yourselves off our land!"

Reuben watched the man. He didn't react at all, not even to look beyond her for any sign of approaching riders. It was as if he knew she was a widow.

"You have money, you will bring it out and hand it to us, or we will torch your barn." The voice was muffled behind the mask, and the man raised his torch high above his head.

Reuben watched as Angelina raised the shotgun, the riders surrounding the speaker doing the same. "This is a small farm, and all our money goes on buying grain to grow crops to feed people. If you want to find a rich farmer, seek out Clement Bolger."

The man on the horse shook his head. "You've had your warning. Now, go fetch your silver or we'll set the barn aflame and maybe your home as well. You got kids, have you? It'd be a shame ... Now I strongly advise you to lower your weapon, darlin'. You got one gun, I got five and you'll go down like a sack of grain if you do."

Reuben glanced at Skeeter and whispered for him to be ready. The leader had a cool enough head, but the other riders looked as nervous as their horses which were shying from the torches held above them.

At a nod from the leader, the rider nearest the barn edged closer to the wall and held out the torch.

Angelina's shotgun followed him and then another rider suddenly raised his pistol, firing a single shot that whistled past Angelina, close enough to her horse to send it into a panic.

The shooter didn't get another chance, pitching from the saddle as Reuben opened fire. Skeeter brought down the one closest to the barn and the leader looked into the copse, searching for the source of the shooting. Then, quite suddenly and without looking back, he turned his horse and rode away, heading for the highway.

"Boss!" Skeeter called out, pointing to where one of the torches had landed by the barn wall, catching almost immediately.

Reuben burst from cover, running for the barn as Angel brought her horse under control and galloped to the fire, slipping off its back and then heading into the darkness as Reuben and Skeeter stamped on it. Moments later, she appeared with a bucket of water which she threw onto the blaze, dampening it down before a second bucket quenched it.

Meanwhile, Reuben kneeled beside the body of the rider Skeeter had killed. He pulled back the mask and sighed. It was a young man — barely into his twenties — who had died from a single shot to the chest. A good shot by Skeeter.

"Oh, my God," Angelina said, looking down at the dead man.

"You recognize him?"

Angelina kneeled and closed the dead eyes. "I don't know him by name, but I know he works for the Bolgers."

Chapter 9

Clem

REUBEN HUNCHED OVER THE kitchen table, glowering as he cleaned his Colt 1911.

"That son of a bitch," Mike said as Angelina finished telling her story. "But what I don't understand is why?"

Angel sipped at her black and ran a hand across her forehead. "I don't know. Well, I guess he figures to scare me into Clem's arms."

"You're right," Reuben said. "Otherwise, why target *that* barn rather than the silo or the house? It's got nothing especially valuable in it, but setting it afire would sure send you a message."

"Clem said I might change my tune by the end of the week. This must've been what he meant."

"Do you want me to handle it?"

Angel swung on him. "And how, exactly, do you fix on doing that? Kill them all single handed?"

"No," Reuben said, surprised by the vehemence of her attack. "I'm not sure, but I figured I'd put the frighteners on them just as they've sought to do to you."

"Then what? They bring Simmons and the rangers in, and you end up dead and they take the farm anyway."

Reuben sighed. "Then, lady, I'm all out of answers. But this must not be allowed to stand."

"And why not?"

"It's not just."

She laughed at that. "Justice? You won't find it here, Reuben Bane, former exciser."

"He's a what?" Mike said, spitting his drink over the table.

Reuben cursed and shot a glare at her, then tried to calm his voice. "I renounced it, Mike, years ago. I am seeking to atone, but I will not be your concern for much longer. My friends and I will be gone tomorrow."

"And you allowed him to come here? Sharing our house? A fugitive from the Foundation?"

Angel leaned back, breathing out heavily. "I believe him to be an honorable man."

"He is that," Skeeter said, slamming his hand on the table. "Could have killed me. Should have, but he pulled me out of the mud and didn't send me away. Neither me nor Asha. He'd move a lot quicker without us, that's for sure, but he made a promise."

Mike's expression didn't change as Skeeter spoke, but Angel leaned across and took his hand. "If he hadn't been here, they'd have burned the barn down. But, anyway, things are as they are." She turned to Reuben. "Clem comes back tomorrow, and you'd best be gone long before he gets here."

"And what of you?"

Angel swallowed, her expression tightening, eyes cast down in defeat. "I will marry Clem Bolger, for Leo's sake."

Mike went to speak when Reuben said, "Where is the boy?"

"He was upstairs when the fight started," Skeeter said, "But I don't know where he went after that. Kinda assumed he was hidin' in his bedroom."

Angel got to her feet and ran up the stairs, before calling out. "No sign of him!"

She ran into the kitchen as Mike said, "Maybe we're overreacting. Leo often goes off for the day. He knows the farm like the back of his hand."

"No," Angel said. "Something's wrong. I can feel it."

"I'll help you search," Reuben said.

Angel nodded and headed for the door but stopped as she heard the sound of an approaching rider.

She ran back to the kitchen window. "It's Clem! He's got Leo!"

Then she turned to Reuben. "Don't do anything unless he threatens my son, okay? Let me handle it otherwise. Do I have your promise?"

Reuben ground his teeth, but nodded and watched her run to the door, her boots thudding on the hallway floor. He listened at the kitchen window as she pulled the door open.

"Leo! Where have you been?"

"Found him on the track to our place, Angel," Clem said.

"Let me have him!"

"Sure."

There was the sound of small boots on the wooden floor. "Oh, thank God. What were you thinking of?"

"Don't be too harsh on the boy," Clem's voice said. "He came to warn me."

"What about?"

"Look, Angel, you know your own business, but you can't go harboring brigands without consequences. I've got a mind to report this to the rangers."

"You son of a ..."

"Now, before you say any more, I advise you to think carefully. I sent Art back to the farm to fetch the boys."

"Once they've taken their disguises off? I know it was you, Clem Bolger!"

A moment's pause.

"Okay, Mrs. Drew," he said. "Let's talk plain, shall we? I'll have this farm. I'd be happier to do it the easy way by making you my wife."

"That's the easy way?"

"Easier. The other way is for me to report this to Mr. Simmons."

"Or I could drop you now!"

"If I don't get home within the hour, Art knows he's to tell the rangers, and you and crippled Mike will burn. But don't worry, I'll take care of little Leo here."

The boy cried out, but Angel's voice immediately shushed him.

"State your offer plain, Clem, between the two of us."

"It's simple enough," Bolger said, triumph obvious in his voice. "You will become Mrs. Angelina Bolger and sign the farm over to me. You'll be a good wife, and you and Mike will live here safe as houses."

"And you, will you be a good husband?"

Clem laughed at that. "You'll get what you deserve. Now, do we have a deal, or do I call the rangers? Come on, you knew this was coming. Let's get it over with."

"Alright."

Clem whooped with joy. "That sure is great! Now, you be a good girl for a week while I arrange a fine wedding, and then you can be as naughty as I like in the bedroom. And not a word of your crazy theory about those bandits. I'll see you."

The door slammed shut and Reuben heard her steps, but by the time she came into the kitchen, he was running to where Lucifer was tied up.

REUBEN TURNED IN THE saddle to look back at the farmhouse in the golden hour after dawn. It was a beautiful place, for sure. There was no sign of Angelina, though Mike had come out in his wheelchair to bid them farewell.

"Where did you go last night?" the old man asked.

"I had words with Clem Bolger."

Mike's face tightened. "What did you do to him? Did you kill him?"

"No, just words. I gave him some gentle instruction on how to treat women. This woman in particular," he'd nodded at the front door of the farmhouse. "Look, Mike, there's no justice for men like him. Angel was right about that. But it would have done you no good if I'd given him what he deserved. I reckon Bolger will find he's bitten off more than he can chew."

"Maybe you're right, but I can't see him letting me stay here for long."

Reuben tightened Lucifer's saddle strap? and looked down at the man. "I don't know about that, Mike. I have extracted a promise that I believe he will keep."

"What promise?"

"To treat you all with respect and kindness."

"Clem Bolger never made a promise he wouldn't break in a heartbeat. What makes you think he'll keep this one?"

"Because I made a promise of my own."

"What?"

"To come back this way when my errand in the east is done. I have told him if I don't find that all is well here, then he will die. I believe I made my point with enough force. I don't like violence, but it is necessary for some men, it seems. Goodbye, Mike."

They shook hands. "Angel was right, you are a man of honor, whatever happened in your past. I'm sorry she's not here to send you on your way, but she does care, you can be sure of that."

"Thank you, I appreciate it. And please convey my sincere thanks to Angel. We all leave this place much better than when we arrived. Physically, at least."

"I will. But you be sure to keep off the main highways, such as they are. Don't underestimate Clem Bolger's stupidity."

With that, Reuben climbed stiffly into the saddle, and they rode away, heading east, parallel to the road they'd arrived on and the Bolger farm.

They rode in silence, each indulging in their own particular regrets at leaving the place. Reuben's mind was full of the woman, and he kept his back to the farmhouse until, finally, he turned again, though he didn't know why.

He saw a figure on a horse, dark against the bright morning sky. It was her. She sat as still as a statue, then she raised her hand in farewell, and he felt his heart pierced to the core.

Chapter 10

CONTAGION

LARRY AND ANTOINETTE CRAFT lived in a small house in what had been the suburbs of Mecklen. Their place was the only survivor on the block, as they'd lived in it since before the aurora, protecting and repairing it as the dwellings around them were abandoned.

Now, they were in the center of a patchwork of small fields that would have looked like a zoomed-out view of a big farm from above. Once each home fell out of use, the Crafts cleared its lot and grew one crop in each, repeating and rotating them as the seasons passed. It was impressive, and provided a surplus that was sold for low prices at the local market. The Crafts didn't become rich, but they somehow managed to flourish after the end of the world, though things had become progressively tougher as the see-sawing climate caused cycles of drought, flood, heat and cold.

Two armed men stood outside the front door. "It's alright, Mitch," Hannah said. "I'll go in on my own. No sense risking both of us." She took the FFP2 mask from the hands of a guard and put it on.

"Are you sure?" Snider said, though his relief was obvious.

Hannah nodded. "We don't know for sure that it's airborne."

"Doctor Neff is inside already, Councilor," the guard said. "She was the one who gave us the masks."

He opened the door, standing back as far as he could, as if simply being in the vicinity posed a risk. And maybe it did.

The door closed quickly behind her as she went inside. The hallway led to a living room with windows on two sides and a skylight above. It was so well kept that she could almost have believed she'd been transported three and a half decades into the past. Except for the lack of a TV.

"Is that you, Hannah?"

She followed the voice, finding the doctor standing at the open door of the main bedroom. It was on the first floor and had a picture window at one end that looked out over the back yard, light flooding into the room.

Hannah held out her hand. "Lois."

Doctor Lois Neff was a tiny woman in her mid-thirties. She'd been born prematurely, just after the second wave, and her mother had died soon after. According to Neff herself, she'd become first a nurse, then a doctor, to honor her mom.

Hannah wouldn't have recognized the training Neff had received as anything like what a medical professional experienced before the fall. Rather than lectures and hospital placements, Neff had learned at the shoulders of surviving doctors and nurses, keeping detailed records that were now collated in the town hall as her legacy.

Thirty-five years her senior, Hannah had thought she'd had it tough in the misogynistic academia of the old world, but Lois Neff, with her diminutive size and blonde hair, had been forced to fight her whole life to be taken seriously. Those she fought with generally didn't make that mistake twice.

"How are they?" Hannah said, her words a little muffled behind her mask.

Lois gestured to the two figures sharing the king-size bed. Even from here, Hannah could see blotches of red on their faces and arms.

"Bad. Breathing trouble, buboes on their lymph nodes. Raging fevers. The whole nine yards."

"So, it is a form of bubonic plague?"

Lois looked at her, bright blue eyes glinting above the surgical mask. "It's a plague that produces buboes, that's as much as I'm prepared to say."

"Do we have any antibiotics?"

"You know we never have enough. I can only synthesize so much. It's the ethyl acetate that's hard to make enough of. But I've given them a dose, and we'll have to wait and see if it works. It could be viral."

"Jeez, I hope not," Hannah said. "Are they conscious?"

"Toni is. Larry got it worse. I'm not sure how much sense you'll get out of her, though. And be careful. If it's viral, the longer you're in there, the bigger the risk. Sit by the window."

Hannah nodded and went inside.

"TONI? ARE YOU AWAKE?"

It was all Hannah could do to keep from recoiling in horror as she got as close as she dared to the woman in the bed. Antoinette Craft was a distorted mockery of the slight, pretty woman Hannah had known for years. Silver and white hair framed her pale face like a halo. In her memory, Hannah heard Toni's infectious laugh, so full of life. And yet, here she was, on the verge of death unless this disease looked worse than it actually was.

Toni's eyes opened slowly, as if her lids were made of lead. "Is that really you, Hannah? I've been dreaming."

"It's me. I won't ask how you're feeling."

"Huh. Not a pretty sight. Worst I've felt since I had COVID all those years ago. Just don't you come any closer, will you?"

Hannah leaned back, inhaling the fresh air coming in through the picture window.

"Any idea where you caught it?"

Hannah saw her friend's eyes lose their focus and begin to close.

"Toni," she said, wishing she could shake the old woman to wake her. "Please, tell me. Where did you get it?"

And, as her eyes closed, she breathed a name.

Hannah gasped, got to her feet and rejoined Lois Neff at the door. "Do what you can, Lois. These people are important."

"Are they any more important than others who need antibiotics? Look, I like them both too, but we don't have enough to go around, and they are ..."

"Old?"

Neff shrugged.

"You've seen what they've done here. The community needs them. And we've completely lost the plot if we choose who lives and dies purely on how old they are. Please."

Lois sighed and looked into the bedroom. "I'll do my best. Do you think I like the fact that we've been caught with our pants down?"

"Of course not, but things are about to get a whole lot worse if what Toni's just told me turns out to be true. This could have spread to everyone who was taken in for questioning."

"What?"

"Look, I've got to go."

"Where?"

"I need to find Branch."

THEY FOUND BRANCH'S BODY in the mayor's office. He'd collapsed in the corner, as if he'd been giving a report to Carver as he was suddenly overcome.

Hannah kneeled by the body, and, wearing a pair of leather gloves, she examined the visible parts of the man's body.

"He knew he had it," she said, talking over her shoulder to Mitch Snider who was standing at the door, hand over his mouth.

"How do you know?"

"He was wearing a scarf to hide his neck. I can see three buboes running along the side of his throat. Not much on his face, but it's so scarred it's likely Carver wouldn't have noticed until the end."

She got up and rejoined Snider who said, "Let's talk outside."

Once they were standing at the top of the stone steps leading to city hall, Snider groaned. "Out of the frying pan ..."

"Be careful what you wish for. We both wanted them gone."

"I can't believe they didn't tell us. How long ago did Branch die?"

"I'm an astrophysicist, not a coroner, Mitch."

"Take a guess, Hannah."

"It's been hours. That much I can say with some certainty."

"So, Branch drops dead in Carver's office, and rather than alerting us, he orders his people to withdraw."

Hannah looked down at the street below. The all-clear had been sounded as soon as the Foundation forces left the city, but it seemed few people dared to venture out for now. "It doesn't matter. He's gone, and we've got to deal with the fallout."

Snider nodded. "Yes, of course. I'll call a council meeting. First thing to do is trace all of the people held in detention."

"Starting with any that are still in the cells. Good grief, Mitch, how long has it been since we last had an outbreak?"

"Not in my time — not like this, anyway. I guess we've been lucky so far."

"Then Espinoza invited the Foundation in. But look, this isn't the time for debates. This is an emergency. You're the mayor, you need to take charge."

Snider puffed out his chest. "Yes, you're right. I'll find the sheriff. We'll have to go into lockdown until we know how many people have got it. What about you?"

"I'm going back to the Crafts' place."

"Why?"

"Because, Mitch, we need to know if antibiotics work on the disease, and I asked Lois to treat Larry and Toni first. It should only take a few hours to know one way or the other. If antibiotics work, then it's bacterial and all we have to contend with is making enough to treat people when they get sick."

"And if they don't work?"

"Then it's a virus of some sort."

"What does that mean?"

She shrugged. "It could be the end of us."

Chapter 11

EVE

ZAK WAITED ON FATHER Ruiz as he and his betrothed sat at a table in the central quadrant of the former university building. The cherry trees were burdened with blossom, and every now and again, the gentle breeze would dislodge a petal and send it floating down to land on the table.

One lodged in Eve's golden hair, and Zak wanted more than anything to be allowed to brush it away, but he knew that if he made any move he'd be admonished.

No, his job was to stand in silence, to come when wanted, and otherwise to remain invisible.

He tried not to let his gaze wander to Eve, who sat with her back facing him, but the alternative was to focus on the fat friar sitting opposite. Fortunately for Zak, Ruiz barely seemed to notice him. He had successfully merged into the background.

He looked into the middle distance, resting his exhausted mind and sore body.

"Boy!"

Zak snapped out of his meditative state to see Ruiz looking at him across the table. A clerical servant straightened up, as if he'd just spoken into the father's ear.

"Sorry, Father."

Ruiz got up from his seat and gestured at Eve. "Take the mistress to her chamber. I have been called away to an urgent meeting."

"Yes, Father," Zak said, excitement washing away his fatigue.

"Once she is safely in the care of the sisters, you will attend to me in the council chamber."

"Father?" Zak said. Then he saw the surprise on the face of the cleric.

"You heard me."

"But honored Father," the cleric said, shielding his voice ineffectually with his hand, "you will have clerical support, as always."

Ruiz nodded. "I know that. I wish for my own independent record," then he looked at Zak as Eve got to her feet. "You hear me, boy? Deliver her to Sister Greer, then attend to me in the council chamber. Bring pen and paper. And remember, you must hand her directly into the sister's care. From your hand to hers. Am I clear?"

"Yes, Father."

"My dear, I will see you shortly," Ruiz said, turning to Eve with a kindly expression.

"Yes, my lord."

Zak watched as the priest strode away with the clearly still confused cleric.

"Will you come with me, my lady?" he said when they'd disappeared.

"The father said to give you this should circumstances like this arise," she said, withdrawing a long, thin leather object from within her sleeve.

Zak took it, thinking it was an ornate pen, but she mimed opening it and he found it was, in fact, an exquisitely decorated knife, as thin as a pencil but with a deadly point.

"What do you want me to do with it?" he gasped.

"Protect me, you idiot!"

Zak breathed out, realization dawning. A young life spent within the twisted corporate mind of the Foundation had led him to believe them capable of anything.

"Which way do we go?"

She shrugged. "You live here, don't you? I come from the orphanage. Now, let's hurry. The father was nervous for my safety, though I can't imagine why. Why are you looking at me like that?"

Because I think you're the most beautiful girl I've ever seen, he didn't say. "Sorry, mistress. The quickest way to the orphanage is across the main courtyard. But..."

"But what?"

"That might not be the safest."

He could see frustration building in her, so he said, "Do you trust me?"

"Of course not! I've only just met you, and you're just a serving boy!"

That insult was like a slap around the face with a wet flannel. "Come on, then," he said, holding out his hand.

He shivered as she took it, and he drew her toward the downward stairs.

"STOP!"

"What is it?" Zak asked. She'd done nothing but bellyache as he'd guided her expertly down the stairs.

"Where are we going?"

"To the kitchens. We can sneak round the back way to the orphanage. Hurry!"

"I'm wearing heels!"

"Then take them off!"

"And walk on these filthy stairs barefoot?"

"It won't kill you. Unless you want me to carry you, that is."

She huffed, but then sat and pulled off her shoes. The staircase was only dimly lit, and her floral scent mixed with the musty, dusty smell of old, worn carpet. She seemed so fragile, so delicate. The definition of feminine to a boy raised on stories of heroes read from the dog-eared, ripped pages of illicit fantasy books.

"What are you staring at?" she said, her acerbic tone cutting through his hormonal haze. She held out her shoes.

"You'll have to carry them," he said, holding up the knife to show he needed both hands free.

She scowled. "Well, I hope you're prepared to tell the father that I tripped down the stairs and broke my neck, then."

With a resigned sigh, he took the shoes and held out his hand to guide her down the stairs.

Pushing the door open, light flooded in along with the aroma of boiling cabbage.

Jacob was the first to spot them. "Hey, Zak!"

Mr. Wong, the chef, swung around from the huge stove. "Boy, what are you doing here?" Then he spotted Eve. "My God, you haven't …"

"No! I'm obeying Father Ruiz."

At that, Wong nodded and gestured at the others. "Don't you have work to do? Leave Isaac to his business."

Eve followed him across the slabbed floor, and he exchanged a resigned look with Jacob as he passed, then held out his hand again when they made it to the door that led into the pantry corridor.

When they were alone, he stopped to catch his breath and hand back her shoes.

"Right, the door to the outside is at the end of this corridor, then the orphanage is directly ahead. Okay?"

She nodded sullenly, breathing heavily.

"I'm sorry for rushing you, but Father Ruiz wants me at this meeting, and he doesn't like to wait."

"I know. He is cruel to you."

Zak blinked in surprise. Had she really said that? "I deserve it, in the main," he said, defensively. She could have been trying to trap him, after all.

She smiled. "I'm ready. Let's go."

He led her to the end of the corridor and put his hand on the door handle, before looking back at her and nodding.

As he opened the door, he was momentarily blinded by the light flooding inside, but he moved out, forcing his eyes open to try and acclimatize quickly.

Then the world turned upside down.

She yelled as he fell sideways, a weight on his chest and something flashed through the air.

He thrust his hand up instinctively, wrapping his fingers around a thin arm. Pain lanced his shoulder, and he heard a scream that he knew to be his voice, even though it seemed disembodied,

Yelling, he kicked out and his assailant grunted and fell sideways.

Zak couldn't feel his left arm, so he fell forward, bearing down on his attacker with nothing more than his body weight.

Nothing more than his body weight and the knife he held in his other hand.

Screams from all around him.

Then darkness.

HE CAME AROUND INTO a melee of voices.

He looked up, then writhed as pain lashed through his shoulder.

"Hold him still!"

Hands pushed his shoulders back; shapes silhouetted against the bright sky.

Then he remembered.

"Eve? Is she ..."

"It's okay," a familiar voice said. "She is with the sisters. I took her while Jacob fetched the sawbone."

His eyes focused on the asymmetrical face of Mr. Wong. "Here, drink this," the chef said, pressing the neck of a bottle to his lips. "More! It will help. It's my finest cooking sherry. Not real sherry, of course, but an adequate substitute."

Things must be serious, Zak thought. Wong was a taciturn man, the words only tumbling out when he was feeling stressed.

"Ah!" The pain was excruciating, but he couldn't move.

"Can't you wait until the liquor takes effect?" Wong asked someone out of sight.

"The longer it takes me to stitch his wound, the more blood he loses," another voice said. "Now hold still."

Zak bit his lip even as he felt the warming effect of the alcohol beginning to work. Three more times, the needle penetrated his skin and then, finally it was over.

The weight left his shoulder and he realized he'd been put on one of the benches that were dotted around the courtyard.

"Careful, boy," Wong said as Zak tried to sit up. "Rip those stitches and Doctor Gunn'll tear you a new one."

Zak felt Wong's hands under his arm pits, supporting him as he sat up. He was twenty yards from the open door to the kitchen and he saw the doctor kneeling, working on something that lay in a pool of blood on the cobblestones.

"Huh, the doctor wanted to work on the son of a bitch who attacked you before he even sewed you up."

"Why?"

"You don't get any answers from the dead, and you can't execute a corpse."

"Thank you, Mr. Wong."

"I look after my own, boy."

Across the courtyard, the doctor shifted around a little, and as he worked, the figure on the cobbles screamed in pain.

"He's not dead then," Wong said. "Soon enough, he'll wish he was."

Then a man in a guard's uniform bent down and lifted the figure effortlessly. Blood soaked the injured figure's white shirt, and his face was almost as pale.

Zak let out a cry of amazement.

"You know him?" Wong said.

"It's Kurt."

Chapter 12

Barber

Zak awoke to find the stern face of Master Sergeant Barber looking down at him, only just stifling a yell of fear as he came out of a nightmare. With the candlelight picking out the pits and scars on his skin, Barber's appearance made him look like one of the monsters Zak had been taught to fear, but, as he looked closer, he saw the man relax and draw back a little.

"I'm sorry to wake you, boy," he said, taking a seat beside the bed.

Zak tried to fit together the events of the past twenty-four hours. He remembered the attack, and being stitched up, but nothing clearly since.

"Where am I?"

"In the infirmary."

That woke him. His eyes widened and he turned his head from side to side, but couldn't see anything beyond the reach of the single candle beside his bed. The infirmary was a separate building near the Foundation headquarters that was reserved for fathers and their senior servants. He'd never heard of a boy like him being tended here.

"Father Ruiz insisted on you being brought here," Barber said, seeing his confusion. "And if he hadn't, I would."

"Kurt?"

Barber's face clouded. "He's alive. Your mistress's stiletto didn't hit a vital organ, but he's lost a lot of blood."

"Why did he do it?" Zak said, instinctively running his fingers over the bandage on his shoulder.

"What do you know about Kurt?"

"Nothing, master. Except he doesn't like me."

Barber grunted. "Yes, the father didn't do you any favors by having you join a cohort that had trained together for weeks. They'd bonded, you see. And then you turn up, and they see the spoiled servant of a shepherd getting preferential treatment."

"Spoiled?"

"Lie back, boy. Lie back," Barber said, pushing gently on Zak's shoulders. "I said that's how they saw you, not how it is. I know what the servants of the shepherds go through, believe me."

Zak hauled himself up onto his elbows, wincing as he stretched the stitches in his shoulder.

"Careful," Barber said. "Father Ruiz has instructed the medics to give you the best care, but if you tear those stitches, you're going to be in a ton of pain."

Nodding, Zak said. "So, it's because I serve the father, that's why Kurt hates me so much?"

"Yes, and he has more reason than most. He was a young child when his father was condemned as a heretic and the Foundation made Kurt watch when they sent him to the fire. He was cast out and his mother abandoned him."

"What happened to him, master?"

"I fell over him in the city. Thought I'd tripped over an animal, but he saved me."

"He what?"

Barber's face creased with a thin smile. "I'd walked into an ambush. He helped me. Looked like an animal and fought like one."

"So, you owed him? That's why you brought him back and trained him?"

Shrugging, Barber said, "He was wounded in the fight, so I found him a place at the orphanage."

"I never saw him."

"He was only there for a few months — you'd left by that time. They cleaned him up, but when they found out who his father was, they were going to cast him out again. I don't have the authority to overrule the shepherds, Zak, but I am the master sergeant, so I took him into training. It was the only way to protect him."

Zak fidgeted, trying to get comfortable as his wound tightened. "I get why he didn't like me, but that doesn't explain the attack, does it? Or is he crazy?"

"Maybe he is. But I don't think it's a coincidence that you were with Father Ruiz's future bride when he caught up with you," Barber said, leaning closer. "Frankly, I don't think you were the true target. She was."

"Why would he want to kill Eve?"

Barber sighed. "He didn't want to; he was ordered to. At least, that's my guess. You were, perhaps, an incentive given to Kurt, a bonus."

"Master, what's going on?" Zak asked. "I feel like I'm in the middle of things that I don't understand."

Grunting Barber said, "I don't have all the answers, but that's not why I'm here." Again, he moved closer. "I said he's alive, but he won't be for long."

"What's going to happen to him?"

"Standard procedure would be for him to be given to the torturers as soon as he's been physically repaired. Then whatever's left of him will be put to the fire."

Zak felt a surge of horror. "Poor Kurt."

"You mean that?"

"Of course. I mean, I know he hates me, but I don't want him to die."

"He tried to kill you, boy."

Zak nodded. "I know, but he's been through enough."

"Here's the odd thing," Barber said, lowering his voice until it was barely above a whisper. "They're not going to torture him — he's going to die tonight."

Zak's mouth opened wide. "I ... I don't understand."

"Neither do I. Unless they know who sent him to kill you and capture the girl. But that's a mystery for another day. I'm here to ask you to do something for me. I have no right to expect you to say yes, but I hope you will."

"Anything, master."

Master Sergeant Barber rubbed his eyes, his exhaustion suddenly obvious. "There's a code among protectors. This isn't the first time one has attacked the other intending to kill, and there would be few indeed of us if every brawl ended with executions."

"Yes, I understand, though I'm not a protector yet, I'm just a trainee."

Barber nodded. "The code applies from the moment you join the cohort. You can pardon Kurt, and he will be released. It will be treated as an internal matter."

"But he was after Eve. What about that?"

"You're right, he was. But whoever has called off the torturers won't want to admit that. They want to keep up the pretense that this is about one trainee protector attacking another. It's in your hands, Zak."

He looked into Barber's ugly, scarred face and saw the concern, even nervousness, there. In truth, he had no desire for revenge on Kurt, but he also didn't want to have to be watching every shadow once he'd been released. He might not be as lucky next time.

"What will happen to him if I ... what would you call it?"

"Invoke the right of pardon? He won't die," Barber said. Then his face fell. "He'll be banished. Probably sent to work on a trading junk. Likely he won't live long, but at least he'll have a chance and he'll die with a sword in his hand."

"Then I'll do it."

Barber put up his hand. "One other thing, before you make your choice. At the moment, you are in Father Ruiz's good graces. He is grateful that you protected his betrothed."

Zak couldn't help but notice the look of — what was it? Disgust? — that passed over Barber's face before disappearing again.

The Master Sergeant continued, "But he will not be happy if you do this. Any reward you might have expected will likely go up in a puff of smoke."

"But you want me to pardon him, don't you?"

"I do. But I don't have the right to order you to. He sure as hell doesn't deserve your mercy. But he doesn't deserve to burn, either. Rest assured, he'll be punished."

Zak sighed. "I will do it. Not because you want me to, but because it's the right thing to do."

"Good lad," Barber said, getting to his feet. He headed to the door and turned with his hand on the lever. "Just don't expect Kurt to be grateful."

Chapter 13

CHATTANOOGA

IT TOOK NEARLY A week for them to make it to Chattanooga, the next waypoint on their journey north and east.

Birmingham, Alabama, lay directly in their path, but what remained of the city had become a cluster of plague-infested slums without law of any sort. So, they'd followed a ridge to the south that had looked down on the former city from the modest peak of Ruffner Mountain. It sat like a poisoned stain on what had once been a rich, green landscape but was now a semi-arid pattern of browns, yellows and dark greens.

Once they were out of sight of Birmingham itself, the ride became pleasant, though slow, and Reuben's mood had lifted a little, as long as he didn't think too much about Angel Drew.

Their slow pace had suited Asha, though he was now fully recovered, looking healthier than Reuben had ever seen him. Angel and Mike had given them plenty of provisions for the journey, so Reuben hadn't been forced to rely on his bush skills to feed them. In fact, his main fear had been the bands of feral dogs and coyotes roaming the more remote parts of the countryside. Whether due to a mutation or just an adaptation to the new, less urban, world, both dingoes and coyotes had become bolder. And, in Reuben's experience, cleverer.

They'd spent one night in a tavern to the south of Chattanooga, and Reuben had talked long into the night with the owner. The city was governed by a civilian mayor, the barkeep said, and was relatively peaceful. The railroads that met here had long gone, but their trackways had remained, and merchant convoys made their way from the east, north and south, though rarely the west.

And so, Reuben had decided to take a chance and enter the city. They needed ammunition — Skeeter, in particular, only had a few rounds left — if they were to cross the remaining miles to their destination, a city called Mecklen in West Virginia. He'd left the two of them hidden in the woods to the south of Route 24. Skeeter had volunteered to go into the city, of course, but, frankly, Reuben didn't want to risk his safety to the young man. He was honest enough. Perhaps too honest.

He felt a weight lift from his shoulders as he rode Lucifer under the former interstate, but immediately felt guilt at that relief, and fear for their safety. The sooner he was out of Chattanooga again, the better. They still had hundreds of miles to cover, assuming that the woman still lived there, and he wasn't forced to search for her.

The tavern-keeper had told him that the city was now confined to the southern quarter of its original extent, and any concerns about finding the gate were banished when he found the end of a long, winding line. From Lucifer's back, he could see that it ended in a wide metal gate that punctuated a fence of wire and steel extending to left and right as far as he could see.

He got down and gave the horse a quick brush as he waited. As the sun climbed in the sky, he felt the heat gathering and poured a little water into his palm for Lucifer to lap at.

After around an hour, he could make out the blue uniforms of police officers near the entrance. In the years since the end of the world, he'd seen fewer and fewer cops as they'd been quickly replaced by vigilantes in the lawless areas and, as time went on, para-military units or resurrected Army battalions. He simultaneously felt the reassurance that there might be a functioning civil authority here while, on the other hand, the fear of knowing that a well-organized police force was unlikely to welcome a former exciser.

He scratched at the wound on his arm under its bandage. He'd left it exposed to the air for the past few days, but reckoned it would be better hidden under a clean binding if he was to get into the city without raising suspicion.

"You look nervous, friend."

Reuben turned to look down at the man behind him in line. He was at least a head shorter than the former exciser and barely reached the eye level of his pack mule. Back in the day, he'd have looked suspiciously, wondering whether he had mutant genes or a form of dwarfism. But he simply returned the smile. "Not really, but thanks for your concern."

"Name's Howie Escalante," the little man said, extending a hand. "What's wrong with your face?"

Reuben accepted the handshake, finding he had a firm, confident grip that reinforced his relaxed demeanor.

"I had plague a year ago," Reuben said, "And the name's Jacob Day." He'd had long enough to come up with a fake name, even though it played havoc with his literal mind, and he resented having to adopt yet another identity. There was no sign of a major Foundation presence here, but their agents got everywhere, so it made no sense to take the risk.

Escalante nodded, then winked. "Good to meet you, Jacob. What's your business here?"

"I seek an armorer. I've been journeying a long time and need to replenish my supply of ammunition."

The little man sucked his teeth. "Never been here before, I guess?"

"Not for many years."

"Well, they don't give ammo away willingly, I'll tell you that."

"I have silver."

Escalante's head bobbed up and down. "Yeah, sure, man like you wouldn't be stupid enough to try and get into the city without money, would he? But still, maybe you'll find the price a little rich for your taste."

"I have no choice."

The little man regarded Reuben closely, as if evaluating him. "Know what I do?"

"Of course not."

"You're a man of little patience, I can see. A direct man. I like that, but take a little advice: hide that until you're inside. The cops here, they look for any excuse to empty your pocket," he said, leaning in close. He smelled of cheap cologne and weed. "But I'm a buyer and seller of fine goods. A merchant."

"Why aren't you part of a convoy? Don't they get easy entry to the city?"

Escalante shrugged. "I'm not exactly a member of the union. My fellow merchants don't like the fact that I undercut them. I'm a man of the people, you see, I only make a small profit, not like them."

"Sure," Reuben said, not believing a word of it. "Well, good day to you." He turned around, judging that he'd reach the gate in another ten minutes or so.

He felt a tap on his shoulder. "Don't be like that. I can help you. We can help each other."

"How?"

"Well, I can get you past the guards."

"How will you do that?"

"I'll tell them you work for me."

"And they'll believe you?"

The grin returned, and Reuben noticed for the first time that Escalante had a tattoo of a small five-pointed star where his neck met his shoulder. "I know them, they know me."

"Why would you do this?"

"A guy can't just help a fellow traveler out?"

Reuben rolled his eyes and tilted his head doubt-fully.

"Ha! You got me! You'll have to pay me, of course."

"I'll take my chances, thanks."

The little man's face suddenly turned serious, and he grabbed Reuben's arm. "You've got no chance my friend. Look, I'll get us through, but you can pay me after, okay? You'll need silver for the guards, though. What have you got? Hacksilver?"

"Bits."

"Oh, you're from out West? Well, here they'll take anything. Ten bits will do."

"Ten?" That was a week's wages for a field worker.

He shrugged. "Offer five, but expect to pay ten. They'll call it an entry toll, but it goes into their pockets, and the guard commander takes his cut. Deal?"

"Why do you insist so much?"

"Because I'm a good soul who doesn't like to see the innocent taken advantage of."

"I'm not innocent."

"Of the ways of the city, I mean. This isn't the open road, things are different and, besides ..."

"Besides, what?"

"They've seen me talking to you, so if you get in trouble, likely I will too."

Reuben glanced at the nearest cop, who was just approaching the woman before them in line, and nodded his agreement.

"Get out of here, we don't allow your kind in the city," the officer said, pushing back.

The woman fell to the ground. Reuben tensed, but felt Escalante's hand grip his arm.

"My family are inside!" she cried, as she looked up at the guard.

"They got a pass, then. You got one?"

She gestured at the entrance. "It's free entry to family! That's the rule."

"You think you know the laws better than me, woman? Now get out of here before I have you dragged away."

Reuben ripped his arm from Escalante's grip, stepped forward and put out his hand to help the woman up. "Ma'am, let me help you."

"What the hell?" the guard said. "You know her?"

Reuben helped the woman to her feet.

"Are you unharmed?"

Her smile made her look twenty years younger, and she blushed.

"I'm fine, thank you."

He turned to the guard, his face hardening again. "How much does a pass cost, officer?"

The guard blinked in surprise, then Reuben saw the greed in his eyes. He looked along the line and lowered his voice. "You got silver, or looking to barter?"

"Silver."

"Hack?"

"Bits."

The guard's eyes rose in the surprise. "You from the West?"

"Yes. I am on Foundation business."

That got his attention. Even in areas that were independent of it, the Foundation's reputation for ruthlessness was universal.

Reuben could read the man's mind. He was suspicious, and evaluating whether he should challenge Reuben to produce proof.

But, after all, if there was one thing Reuben Bane knew it was how to intimidate in the name of the Foundation.

"I will give you ten bits for my pass and one for this lady."

"Ten?"

"Or call across your commander, and we'll discuss this with him before I write my report on how things stand in Chattanooga."

The guard flushed. "There's no need for that, master. Ten bits would be sufficient."

He reached into the saddlebag and, being careful to shield it from the guard, he took the money from the purse inside. It was a lot lighter than it had been when he'd left New Haven, he would have to negotiate with the armorers if he was to get what he needed without being beggared.

"Here. Give the lady her pass," he said, handing over the octagonal silver pieces. "And know that I will be checking in on her before I leave. If I find that any evil has befallen her, I will look for you. Understood?"

The guard nodded nervously. "I understand, master, though surely there are many perils in the city?"

"You'd better hope she doesn't encounter any, then."

And, with that, the guard stepped back and Reuben led Lucifer through the gate and into Chattanooga.

Chapter 14

INFECTION

HANNAH WALKED THE SILENT streets of Mecklen, trying desperately to find a sliver of hope in the situation. The only positive thing that had happened since the plague arrived in the city was the fact that Toni Craft was still clinging on somehow. Her husband had succumbed to the mysterious disease a few hours after Hannah had first visited them, and both she and Doctor Neff had expected Toni to follow quickly. And yet she still drew breath.

Hannah had spent the day helping Neff as she struggled to cope with the burden of caring for the sick, all the time knowing that the only alternative to allowing it to burn out with devastating consequences for the city, was to find a treatment.

Penicillin had no obvious effect, at least not in the short term. That didn't conclusively prove that the pathogen was a virus, but it was the most likely hypothesis, so they'd taken it as a working assumption. The antivirals left over from the age of COVID had been used up decades before, and there was no way to manufacture them even if their chemical structure was known. Penicillin, after all, was basically everywhere — it was a matter of concentrating and purifying it, and Doctor Neff was the only person who'd successfully set up a crude process for creating and harvesting it. And even that, it seemed, was useless.

She looked up at the darkening sky as the first stars began emerging, half expecting to see an aurora, then chided herself. There was no more chance of one tonight as at any other time, it just seemed that the universe was apt to kick humanity in the nuts when it was already on the ground. No, that wasn't scientific thinking.

Hannah could see candles burning in windows and nervous faces looking out. Were they simply curtain-twitchers wondering why she was out during lockdown? Or did they think she was going to knock on their door and bring the plague inside?

She'd certainly been around plenty of sufferers — over a hundred had come down with it so far — but she'd taken every possible precaution.

She didn't have the plague.

Though her legs felt leaden as she strode along, exhaustion threatening to overwhelm her.

Hannah put her hand inside her jacket and felt her armpit.

Nothing.

Except that it was tender to the touch. The lymph node.

Suddenly, the half mile to her cottage seemed like an unimaginable gulf as panic flooded her body. She picked up the pace, almost stumbling as she tried to cover the distance before the increasing weakness in her legs made it impossible.

Or was she just having a panic attack?

She found she was second- and third- guessing herself and just repeating over and over again a desperate prayer simply to make it.

And she did.

It felt as though she was using the last ounce of her strength to open the door. This would be a good time for Roberto to turn up.

But he wasn't there.

Dammit, he never got sick. He could look after her.

But he wasn't there.

She slammed the door behind herself and staggered to the bedroom, hauling herself up the stairs as if the banister were a tug-of-war rope.

The cool, dark of the bedroom soothed her skin as she abandoned her clothes and made her way into the bathroom. She washed her face and used the bucket before finally collapsing onto the bed.

IT WAS THE FOLLOWING day when she woke up. Or had she slept through more than one night?

She rolled onto her back and explored the lumps on her armpits. Bigger and sorer. Then she felt along her neck, crying out in pain as she felt something wet on her fingers.

If only Roberto was here.

He'd looked after her before, and she yearned to see his disfigured face looking down on her in obvious concern.

And she knew he wouldn't get the plague; he was immune to viruses.

He was immune to viruses.

There was something in that.

Not just that he wouldn't be able to get the plague.

She felt consciousness slip away, but fought against the oblivion her body wanted so badly.

Her mind was so sluggish. She knew she'd just thought of something significant, but couldn't grasp it.

And she needed sleep so very badly.

But as she felt the darkness return, she saw his face looking down on her.

"*It's okay, Mom. I won't catch it.*"

"*Remind me to take a blood sample when I'm better. I need to get to the bottom of this.*"

She woke up, fell out of bed, knowing that she'd had some kind of revelation, went to get up off the floor and remembered no more.

***

"HANNAH! WAKE UP HANNAH."

She forced her eyes open, pushing against the mattress and rolling over. Where was she?

In her bed.

How had she gotten here?

She remembered, what? Falling.

Yes, she'd fallen out of bed.

She'd had something to do.

And now she was here.

"Hannah, can you hear me? Hannah, it's me, Lois. Doctor Neff."

"Doctor who?"

It was the snigger that finally brought her back to awareness.

"No, Doctor Neff."

She looked up to see the younger woman's blue eyes peeking at her from behind a mask.

"You're not dead, then," the doctor continued. "When I saw you on the bed, I thought the worst."

Hannah groaned. "I feel like death." The truth was, however, that she felt a subtle lightness to her limb and head that she wasn't expecting.

"I was worried about you. You looked pretty drawn when you left, but I figured you'd been working too hard at ..." She stopped herself.

"At my age?"

Lois nodded. "Something like that. But you don't look like giving up the ghost just yet. In fact, the buboes don't seem to be swelling."

"What day is it?"

"Wednesday. I saw you last two days ago. I didn't have time to check in on you until now."

"What?" So, she'd slept for thirty-six hours.

Lois looked to the side of the bed. "What's the last thing you remember?"

She tried to think, but her brain was foggy. "I fell off the bed."

"And yet, here you are. I certainly didn't lift you."

Roberto? No, she'd remember if he'd returned, surely?

"Then you won't know why you've got a syringe on your bedside table?"

"A what?"

Lois's head moved out of sight and then returned again holding up a small bottle.

"Who is Roberto?"

She turned the bottle, and she gasped as she saw his name and remembered what she'd done.

"So, LET ME GET this straight, you injected plasma into your bloodstream?"

"No. I'd noticed that Roberto's granulocyte count was off the chart, and hypothesized that this was why he never suffered from any viral infection, even when we were in close proximity."

She'd managed to make it down to the kitchen, and was sitting at a chair while Lois Neff fired up the wood-burning stove and put the kettle on top.

"Well," the diminutive doctor said, "you've either experienced a near miraculous spontaneous recovery, or whatever you injected worked. If it's the latter, there's hope for us all. But, good grief, it was a hell of a risk, Hannah."

Hannah sat with her head in her hands, feeling as though it was too heavy for her neck to support and regretting getting out of bed. "I wasn't thinking straight, or at all. It was as if I was drunk, I had no filter, nothing warning me that it might not be a good idea."

"Whatever it was, it probably saved your life."

A mug of hot tea appeared on the table and Hannah smiled. "Ironic. I'm the least impulsive person I've ever known. Except Mitch, maybe. What?"

"He came down with it yesterday. I'm going to see him next, though there's not much I can do. There's a little left in the vial, but I don't think he'd let me use it on him."

"You'd be surprised," Hannah said. "Sorry, no, you're probably right."

"And even if I did, and it saved him, we've got well over a hundred sick people now... Look, Hannah, you've got to tell me. Who is this Roberto? And where can we find him?"

Chapter 15

SHANA

REUBEN FELT AS THOUGH his ears were under assault from the cacophony that greeted him as he walked into Chattanooga. Beyond the gate was a thoroughfare that swept from right to left, though he had no idea where it led. Most people walked, but he saw horses, mules and donkeys being led by their owners. It was only now, after thirty-five years, that pack-animals were becoming relatively common, their ancestors having been taken below ground with their owners when the second wave hit.

It had been a long time since Reuben last shared a space with so many people, all, it seemed, with something to say to one another. There was an energy to it that, though he felt momentarily uncomfortable, reminded him of the distant past, when crowds like this were the norm.

Instinctively, he wanted to put his hands over his ears but, even more, he wished he could block out the stench of many humans without sophisticated deodorant in a small, hot place. Lucifer, by contrast, waited patiently alongside as the crowds swept past them, but Reuben had long guessed the horse was getting a little deaf. Or had developed selective hearing.

He felt a tug on his arm. "Thank you, sir."

It was the woman he'd helped. "That's quite al-right. I don't like bullies."

"Do you have somewhere to stay?"

"I don't. I only intend to be in the city for a brief time. I thought, perhaps, I'd find a hostelry."

She shook her head. "You'll come and stay with my family, if you will. You and your fine beast. My name's Lily, Lily Dillard."

"I am," he began, then just caught himself, "Jacob Day. And thank you."

If anything, she looked a little disappointed. Per-haps she'd been hoping he'd refuse, and her obliga-tion would be satisfied without any inconvenience. "Can I ask, were you telling the truth about being on Foundation business?"

"No. I've dealt with men like that often enough to know how to handle them."

The relief was obvious. "That's good."

"Jacob, have you forgotten me?"

He turned to look down on the little merchant, Es-calante, who'd brought his pack mule alongside Lu-cifer. In truth he had, indeed, forgotten, and hadn't watched the man come inside the city.

"My offer still stands," he said. "Trust me, you don't want to go to the official armorers, they'll fleece you. Unless you're made of money, that is."

Reuben thought about the lightness of his purse and sighed inwardly. "Thank you, I would appreciate a guide."

"Well, you go about your business, Mr. Day," Lily said, "and come to Chestnut Street when you're done. I'll make us a meal to celebrate."

He smiled and shook her hand. "Thank you, lady. It will be good to sleep in a bed tonight."

Reuben watched her go, then returned to the merchant. "What is this going to cost me?"

Escalante had the grace to flush, but quickly shook it off. "I'll take a small percentage, that okay?"

"I don't care what you skim off the top, as long as the man does good work at a price I can afford."

"Oh, I think you'll be happy enough. What are you looking for?"

"Thirty-six caliber balls and number ten caps."

Escalante nodded. "Sure, sure, no problem."

"And forty-five ACP."

"You got a Colt?"

Reuben nodded. "I do."

"Original? Working?"

Reuben nodded again.

"Don't tell no one else, that's my advice."

"Do you think the armorer will have some?"

Escalante sucked his teeth. "Maybe. Ain't made any more, as far as I know."

"Then let's ask."

The merchant looked around the square. "Well, I don't know about you, but I could do with a bite to eat."

"Take me to the armorer, or I'll go my own way."

Putting on an offended expression, Escalante shrugged. "Suit yourself, but you owe me a meal. I know a place that does the best enchiladas in the world."

THE ARMORER WORKED OUT of a small shop in Houston Street. Judging by the faded paint on the inner walls, it had once been a mechanic's workshop, but the automobiles had given way to what, frankly, looked like an utter chaos of tools scattered over benches, and finished metal objects on racks.

"Hey, it's me!" Escalante called out, waving his hands as he edged inside the open front. "It's your friend, okay? Old Howie."

Reuben, who was tying Lucifer to a rusty railing, watched the pantomime and wondered what he was getting into.

He saw Escalante go stiff as his head turned. "There you are! You can put the gun down, I'm here on business. Got a client for you." He paused as if listening, then turned his head in Reuben's direction while keeping his hands raised. "Come closer, my friend."

Reuben patted the Navy pistol on the inside of his jacket and edged nearer to the little man's back.

He saw the barrel of a shotgun emerge into the sunlight. "Raise your hands, real slow. I got a chamber full of nailshot that'll rip you to shreds however fast you move."

Reuben raised his hands as the armorer emerged. "You're a woman."

"Sharp one you've brought me, How. If he's rich as well, then you've hit the jackpot for once. Name's Shana — didn't he tell you?"

Escalante relaxed and smiled. "I wanted to keep it a surprise."

The shotgun barrel waved in the direction of a bench near the entrance. "You can put your weapons there, and then we'll do the introductions, okay?"

Reuben stepped to the bench and deposited the Navy revolver, then removed the knife from his belt and dropped it alongside.

The armorer glanced quickly. "1851 Colt Navy, cap and ball. Reproduction, of course, but not recent. My guess, twenty-twenties, Pietta."

"All correct, except I don't know when it was made exactly."

She lowered the shotgun and drew a small pistol from her belt. "I ain't a great shot on account of my eyesight, but I'll hit you from here if you make any moves that offend me, you understand?"

He nodded.

"That Navy cost you a pretty penny, am I right? Could have gotten five modern ones for the same money."

Reuben shrugged. "A gun needs to be reliable and accurate to be worth anything."

A smile spread over her face. She was a compact woman of indeterminate age without an ounce of fat. She wore a white T-shirt under blue denims and an ancient baseball cap with a pair of glasses perched on top. "Ah, a man who knows his weapons."

"You ain't heard nothing yet," Escalante said, unable, it seemed, to contain himself. "He's got a Colt."

"You have? Genuine?"

Reuben nodded. "Indeed. 1911 Government. I inherited it from a good friend who'd been a cop on the West Coast. He showed me how to use it."

"Where is it?"

"Outside the city with my comrades." Both of whom were under strict instructions not to touch it except in an emergency.

The armorer nodded, smiling at the little merchant. "I take it back. I can see I'm dealing with a professional."

"Do you have any forty-five ACP?"

"Original? Maybe I know where I can get some, but the kind of customer who comes to me instead of the official armorers isn't likely to be rich enough."

Reuben grunted. He'd never had much of a problem getting original ammunition when he was a Foundation exciser, but as soon as he had to fend for himself, he'd found out how precious original rounds were. Those that weren't in Foundation armories had generally found their way into the hands of the various governments trying to establish themselves, or independent military units. Some were available on the black market, but, as Shana had said, they were ruinously expensive.

"Ah, but you have a solution, don't you, my volatile friend?" Escalante said, nudging her.

She glanced at the little merchant, then back at Reuben. "Yeah. You see, the problem isn't the cartridges themselves, I can make them or repurpose spent cases. The problem is the propellant. Rumor has it the Foundation's got a plant making it, but otherwise white powder's just not something the likes of me can get ahold of."

"So, what have you done?" Reuben asked, becoming irritated by the slow unwinding of the armorer's thoughts.

"Simple. I use black powder. You don't get the power of an original and it lets out a heap of smoke, but it gets the job done, that's for sure."

"And my weapon will take it?"

She nodded, eagerly. "Sure. You'll need to keep it extra clean, but I guess someone like you does that anyway. And, like I say, you won't get as much range. But a 1911 with my cartridges will still beat that Navy revolver any day, let alone the crap they're making today. You'll keep your edge, my friend, or, at least, most of it."

"Thank you. How much will it cost?"

"Well, that depends on how much you want to spend and how long you're willing to wait for me to make it."

"I wish to leave the city tomorrow."

She rubbed her chin, shaking her head. "I can let you have what you need for the navy revolver, say a hundred rounds in total, tomorrow. I got twenty rounds of the ACP, but I could probably make another thirty by this time tomorrow. If the price is right."

Reuben went back to Lucifer and retrieved his purse, leaving a few bits loose in the saddlebag.

The armorer took the purse, weighed it in her hand, regarded him closely, then nodded. "You know, I could charge twice this for what I'm making, but I kinda like the idea of my handiwork in the hands of a professional. You seem to me to be a man with a mission and I'm betting that the authorities wouldn't exactly approve."

Reuben gave a slight smile and shook the armorer's hand. And went away practically penniless.

Chapter 16

LILY

"I'M SORRY," REUBEN SAID. "This takes advantage of your offer, but ..."

Lily, the woman he'd helped to get into the city, stood at the door and looked beyond Reuben to the figure of Escalante. "He has nowhere to stay?"

"There's no room at any of the inns," the merchant said, bobbing up and down, rubbing his hands. "And the curfew starts in ..."

"Half an hour."

"Again, I'm sorry," Reuben repeated. "If I could afford it, I'd find us a room, but my business today has left me without the means."

The woman shook her head. "Wait here." She disappeared, and Reuben was left on the doorstep to glower at Escalante until she returned again. "Okay, but you'll both have to sleep in the living room and there's only one couch."

"That's quite alright, ma'am," Escalante said, bobbing again. "It'll be a luxury to sleep on an actual floor rather than rocks and dirt."

She ignored him. "You can take your horse into the back yard and tie him up. I'll meet you with some water for him."

"Thank you, ma'am."

Lily headed back into the house, and Reuben grabbed the merchant's shoulder as he went to follow. "I don't know what your game is, Escalante," he hissed. "Quiet! I'm speaking. You will treat this house and the people inside with respect. Do you understand me? She's let you in because of me, so you're my responsibility. Let me down and you'll regret it."

He pushed the merchant into the house, then led Lucifer around the side, where Lily met him with a watering can she used to fill a trough. Reuben let Lucifer drink, and then fed him some grain.

"You're a strange man, Jacob" Lily said as she watched him tend his horse. "I reckon you're a compassionate man – you helped me out in the line earlier. But I also sense conflict. It's as if you have a raging torrent inside. I wouldn't want to be around when the dam breaks."

"I'm fine. I promise that nothing will happen while I'm under your roof."

"I believe you. Now, come and meet my family."

She led Reuben in through what had been a frame for a sliding glass door which had been replaced with shutters that rolled back.

An older man with a big, well-kept salt and pepper beard approached as he went inside, hand held out. "So, this is our hero, is it? I thought at first that it was this man," he said, gesturing to where Escalante stood, smiling sheepishly, "but I know him, and he is no hero. You, on the other hand, now here is a man who knows what is right."

Reuben, taken aback by the energy of the man, meekly accepted the outstretched hand.

"And you have a fine beast. A little long in the tooth, I think, but aren't we all? Jacob, that's your name, isn't it? Did my Lily get that right?"

A lie repeated is a lie compounded, Reuben thought, but he simply nodded. "She got it right, sir."

"I am Adam, and you are welcome in my house. This is my son Benjamin," he said, gesturing at a younger man who was lurking near Escalante, "and his wife Natalie, and their children are here somewhere."

Reuben exchanged greetings with Benjamin and Natalie, and then followed Lily to the table, waiting until the others sat before taking his seat.

"Natalie has made us a wonderful meal to celebrate Lily's return. And she has baked us this fresh bread."

Reuben's stomach gurgled as he saw the brown loaf.

"Do you mind if I say a prayer, Jacob?"

"No, father!" Lily said, a hint of fear in her voice. "We don't wish to offend our guest."

"You are a religious man?" Adam said.

Reuben shook his head. "Do not concern yourself about offending me. I'm in your home. Please, behave as you normally would."

Lily didn't respond when Adam looked for confirmation from her, so he simply raised his open hands and said, "*Barukh ata Adonai Eloheinu, melekh ha'olam, hamotzi lehem min ha'aretz*. There, short and sweet."

"I appreciate your trust," Reuben said as Natalie handed a plate to him. The smell was so delicious it was all he could do to stop himself drooling. It was a meatloaf of some kind, and he'd been given the largest slice.

"Ah, it's nothing. If the Foundation had spies in every home, then there would be many burnings, not just of my people. They tolerate nothing but Foundation dogma, so we are treated no worse than our Muslim brothers and sisters, or Catholic, Baptist or Pentecostal. But here in Chattanooga, we do not fear them."

Reuben grunted. "You should, Adam. You should. Trust no one, especially strangers. You have children here."

"That is true enough, my friend," Adam said as he offered the loaf and bread knife to Reuben. "But I know a like mind when I meet one."

"Father!"

"Oh, hush, my son," he said, jabbing a finger at Benjamin. "Trust my instinct, it has always served us well."

Reuben looked from one to the other. "If it means anything, I will swear to you that nothing you say will go beyond this room. At least, not from my lips."

He glanced over at the merchant who was cutting a slice of bread to go with his meatloaf.

"Ah," the man said, "this conversation becomes a little rich, unlike this fine meatloaf. With your permission, I'll eat it in the yard and check on my friend's horse."

With that, he got to his feet and disappeared, leaving Reuben alone with Adam and the others.

The meatloaf was as delicious as it looked and smelled, and Reuben found himself relaxing as he enjoyed his first good meal since he'd left Angel Drew's farm.

He refused seconds and sat back with a sigh. "Thank you, Mrs... Dillard?"

Benjamin's wife — a dark-haired woman with a pleasant smile — chuckled. "Dillard was Lily's name. She married outside the community. I am Natalie Rogan. And you are welcome."

With Lily and Benjamin's help, she cleared the table and then went to check on the children. When she returned to the table she said, "Your friend is asleep."

Reuben was going to deny that the merchant was any friend of his, but knew this was churlish. And he'd had a good meal, after all. And Benjamin had brought over a dark liquor in a bottle with a torn and faded Jack Daniels label.

"Thank you, Mrs. Rogen. I'll bring him inside presently."

"So, Jacob," Adam said, pouring a measure into a whiskey glass, "what brings you to Chattanooga, if it is permitted to ask."

Reuben thanked the man and raised his glass. "Of course. I am traveling to West Virginia."

"Where from?"

"The west. Nevada."

Adam's eyes widened. "You have crossed the Western Desert?"

"I was well provisioned."

"And you've had the plague, I see."

"Father!" Lily snapped.

"Oh, shoosh. The man knows we can all see the scars. We are adults here."

Reuben smiled at Lily. "It's okay. I am not a vain man and the physical scars are merely a reminder of what, and who, I lost to the plague."

Those words hung in the air, but even Adam didn't seem willing to poke that particular wound. "Where in the West did you set out from?"

"A place called New Haven. They cared for me, and, in payment, I undertook this mission."

"You have been to New Haven?" Benjamin said, suddenly animated. "What is it like?"

Reuben glanced at Adam, who'd given his son a warning look, but too late. "You've heard of it?

"We have," Adam said. "Long story, for later."

"Well, thirty-five years ago, it was an unremarkable town like thousands of others. Now, it survives despite everything the world, and people, throw at it. How long it can keep going, I don't know. The desert will swallow it one day."

"What did they ask you to do?"

Adam raised his hand. "No, my son, our friend must be allowed to keep his secret. It must be important, or he would not have been sent across two thousand miles."

Was it, though? Reuben wondered. Former mayor, Desmond Myers, had set him the task when Reuben had asked if there were any way he could repay the town. But it had seemed to him that this was personal for Myers, so perhaps, in the grand scheme, it was meaningless.

Not to Reuben, though. It was repayment of a debt.

Either way, he didn't want to talk about it.

"Have you heard about Washington?" Benjamin asked.

"DC?"

"Washington State."

"What about it?"

Benjamin glanced around the room in case there might be someone hiding in the shadows. "The Army has taken control of Seattle."

"Which Army?"

"Now that, my friend, is a good question," Adam said, pouring a second drink for himself, Benjamin and Reuben. With a scowl, Lily took the bottle and poured one for herself.

"Let me ask you this," the old man continued. "How many, what shall we call them, unitary authorities are there in North America, now?"

"You mean, governments? Dozens, maybe hundreds."

Adam wagged his finger. "No, I mean bigger. When you and I were young, there was the Federal government, wasn't there? How many like that?"

"There's Texas," Reuben said, counting on his fingers, "they've been independent since the first wave. There's the Foundation Territories."

"Yes, and they swell like a disease. They control much of the East Coast and inland, and isolated parts of the rest of the country. They hope, one day, to be *the* government."

"Good luck convincing Texas of that," Reuben said.

Adam smiled. "So, that is Texas and the Foundation Territories. There's also the Federal Government, of course. They control the East Coast south of DC, but I wonder how independent they are?"

"They're irrelevant," Benjamin said. "A dying rump."

"No, son, they are not. They still have control of much of the country's armaments. If they wanted to, they could nuke us all."

Reuben nodded. "They are increasingly in the Foundation's pocket."

"Yes, indeed. So apart from some individual states who, at present, pay lip service to the Federal Government — like West Virginia — that is the East. But what of the West."

Shrugging, Reuben said, "LA has some authority locally, but the other cities have all been swamped by the sea, except Vegas which has disappeared under the sand. I hadn't heard of anything happening in Washington."

"Lily, my dear, will you check that our friend is still sleeping in the yard?"

Reluctantly, she got to her feet and headed out.

Adam watched her go and leaned closer to Reuben. "We must be a little careful. I know your friend; he is a merchant and merchants care only about money. I know, I was one for many years."

Lily returned, nodded and sat down again.

"Come, will you follow me?"

Surprised, Reuben drained his glass and stood, feeling a little unsteady. It was strong liquor. He fell in line behind Adam as they climbed the stairs. "We must be quiet," the older man said. "The children are asleep."

He went to one of the five doors and opened it. It was a perfectly ordinary bedroom until Adam pushed aside a stack of books on a shelf and pulled forward a radio receiver.

"We have used this to keep in touch with our friends across the country. The last time we heard from Seattle, it was under attack. And then our friend went silent, and we haven't heard anything from him since."

"What happened?"

Adam shook his head. "He said they were regular Army, and he's old enough to remember what they looked like in the old world. Not some thugs playing dress up, but trained infantry and artillery.

"The city had its own administration, though many districts were still uninhabited and other parts were underwater. Our friend doesn't have any idea where the invaders came from, but they took the city by surprise and only the area around the administrative center put up any resistance."

"Weird," Reuben said. "They came out of nowhere?"

Adam nodded. "And that's not the worst of it. Our friend said there were rumors of an elite unit that cleared out the last resistance and didn't leave a single man or woman alive."

"I don't listen to rumors. If no one survived, how could there be any witnesses?"

"I do not doubt my friend's account any more than I doubt the word from New Haven."

Ice poured into Reuben's gut. "What?"

Adam smiled. "Yes, we were told to watch out for a man heading for West Virginia on a mission for them. His name was Reuben Bane, and he was once an exciser."

Reuben opened his mouth to speak, but was interrupted by a thumping sound coming from the front door. He ran over to a window that looked out on the street.

"Police," he said.

Chapter 17

ESCALANTE

REUBEN CROUCHED IN THE bedroom doorway, listening to the voices from below. At first, he'd thought he must have been betrayed by Adam and his family, but he'd seen no indication in their faces, and Adam had looked genuinely fearful as he made his way downstairs.

Benjamin had bundled the radio receiver into place behind the books — a pathetic disguise, but he'd had no time for anything else.

"You took your time," the voice said.

"Hello officer, I'm sorry, I was upstairs," Adam said. "It is our house rule that only I open the door after curfew."

A second voice said, "We're looking for a fugitive."

Reuben got ready to run. Adam had said he could climb through the shutters in the children's bedroom if he had to.

"No criminals here, officer," Adam said, in a relaxed and confident voice.

"Well, he was last seen in this street, so we have to check. His name's Escalante. Do you know him?"

Reuben didn't hear the response as he breathed out in relief. But then he remembered that the little man was in the back yard. If he was found here, the Rogans would likely be charged with hiding him.

The next thing he heard was the sound of booted feet coming in through the front door, so he crept into the children's bedroom and opened the shutters before climbing onto the ledge. He could see directly down into the back yard. There was Lucifer, but Escalante's mule was gone and there was no sign of the merchant.

Then he heard footsteps coming up the stairs. If he was found here, then that would lead to awkward questions and, again, land the family in a heap of trouble if his true name and nature was revealed.

He braced himself to jump down into the yard then, quite suddenly, the sound of a whistle penetrated the darkness.

"They've got him!" a voice from downstairs called, and the footsteps turned and left. Reuben was about to climb inside when he thought: what if Escalante had drawn the police away so the Rogans and their radio wouldn't be discovered? What if he also knew that Reuben wasn't what he claimed to be?

Likely enough, he'd just run for it when he heard the police to save his own skin, but Reuben had to know.

So, holding his breath, he jumped down to the backyard and rolled sideways, grimacing at the pain in his knees as he hit the ground.

He yearned to climb on Lucifer's back and go, but that would make him far too obvious. "I'll be back, boy," he said, patting the horse's rump and then, just as the last of the police officers left the house, he darted over the back fence and into the night, following the sound of the whistle.

REUBEN RAN ALONG THE dark streets, eyes and ears straining for the cry to go up. The whistle had stopped, but he had a hunch as to where Escalante might have headed, so he was taking the direct route.

If he was in the merchant's position, he'd be heading for Shana, the armorer, on the basis that she was probably the most dangerous person he knew. And, besides, she was the only person Reuben knew apart from the Rogens, and he wasn't going back there in a hurry.

There was no street lighting, so the Chattanooga authorities either hadn't figured that out or they didn't waste power after curfew. Behind the shutters and surviving windows of the houses he passed, the orange glow of flickering candles and oil lanterns made for a dim illumination so he could see his feet.

Within moments, he was panting. He hated being old. He should be enjoying a well-earned retirement, but his conscience had gotten in the way, so here he was, running along the sidewalks of a city he didn't know in an attempt to rescue a man he didn't like and who probably didn't deserve it.

He stopped for a moment, breathing heavily, to check his surroundings. Behind him, he saw a hint of running feet. So, he'd gotten ahead of the cops by taking a direct route, but they were close behind.

Taking a deep lungful of air, he ran on, his Navy revolver in his right hand, glad that the curfew was keeping people off the streets and making navigation easier.

Then he saw a figure slumped against a wall with a cop standing over him. The officer was peering over his shoulder, looking for his comrades to arrive, and Reuben was only just in time to dart behind a wall and escape notice.

He hefted the pistol, waited for the cop to look away and ran at him as silently as he could manage. The cop turned just as Reuben swung the weapon, knocking him to the ground instantly.

"Jacob! Is that you?" Escalante said. He'd been crouching on the floor, but scrambled to his feet as he recognized Reuben.

Bane grabbed his arm to steady him. "Where can we hide? Are you heading for Shana's?"

"I couldn't think of anywhere else!"

"Come on, then. And we'd better not lead them to her door, or she'll kill the both of us."

They scampered along the wall and turned the corner just as the cry went up from behind them. The cop's body had been found.

"Did ... you ... kill ... him?" the little merchant said, panting.

"I don't think so."

Reuben stopped at the next corner and peered behind them, his breath misting in the scattered orange glow of the nearest house. "Look, you'd better level with me. Why are they after you?"

"Search me."

Reuben shook him by the shoulders. "Tell the truth!"

Escalante shrugged before glancing back the way they'd come. "I don't know why they want me."

"You mean, it could be many things? You just don't know what they want you for this time?"

"Something like that, but it doesn't matter, does it?"

"It matters because we need to know whether they'll turn the city upside down to find you."

Escalante tugged at Reuben's arm. "We'd better go. This isn't the first time I've had them after me. They stop soon enough, then I pay the right people, change how I look, and they forget me completely. Well, for a while, anyway."

REUBEN ALLOWED THE LITTLE man to lead the way, noticing he was taking a circuitous path that would lead them past the street containing Shana's workshop before approaching it from the north.

By the time they made it, the sounds of pursuit had died away entirely, and they'd slowed their pace a little.

"Good, she's in," Reuben said, pointing at the light leaking from one of the workshop windows.

Escalante chuckled. "She's always in. Now, we gotta be careful she realizes it's us."

Reuben followed him as the merchant approached the workshop door, but before he could touch the handle, a voice called out.

"I know you're there. You'd better get inside. My trigger finger's awful itchy."

She was behind the counter, scowling as Escalante made his way inside. Her mood brightened a little when she saw Reuben.

"You should be more careful about the company you pick," she said.

Reuben grunted. "Right enough."

"I heard the whistle, then I saw him running my way."

"How?"

She pointed at the ceiling. "I got my ways of keeping an eye on what's going on. Pretty much essential in my line of work, you know?"

"What am I going to do, Shana?" Escalante said.

"Why should I care?"

His face creased up in fear. "But it's my third strike!"

"Why should I give a damn about that?"

"We're friends! I've brought you business over the years. I mean, there's Jacob here. You've made a killing from him."

Shana's face tightened. "I could have charged twice as much and still been cheaper than the official armorers. But, yes, I suppose you've been useful. You want my advice?"

"Yes!"

"Go and jump off a tall building."

"Shana!"

"No? Well then, I advise you to get out of the city as fast as your little legs can run."

"Where do I go?"

"Not my problem."

"More importantly," Reuben said. "Is there a way out we can attempt?"

Shana took out a cigarette and lit it, before offering one to Reuben who shook his head.

"The only way that isn't watched is southwest."

"The trash dump?" Escalante said, eyes wide. "We can't go that way!"

"We?"

"You have to take me with you!" the merchant said, turning on Reuben.

"I don't have to do anything."

Shana shrugged. "You kinda do. Should have left him to the cops if you wasn't going to help him escape."

"Tell me about the trash dump," Reuben said, with a sigh. Two weeks ago, he'd been responsible for no one but himself, but he seemed to be picking companions up like a flytrap. Still, he could jettison the little man as soon as they were clear of the city.

"Nothing much to say. It stinks to high heaven — dangerously on still days — and, as far as I know the only people who live there are the garbage surfers. Desperados and muteys."

"Deviants? Why doesn't the city clear them out?"

"Because then they'd have to patrol that section. This way, they get to keep folks out while penning their trash in one place."

"Human trash?"

Shana shrugged. "I didn't say that. Probably how the city sees them, though. There's rumors that they eat trash and, sometimes, folks who wander in." She paused for a moment as if weighing him up, then nodded. "You'll be alright. And I guess you want to know how far I got with your order?"

"You've started?"

"Thirty ACP cartridges. Give me ten minutes and I'll get your percussion supplies ready. I'm guessing you don't have much powder?"

Reuben shook his head. "I'm grateful, Shana."

"Well, it's a shame our friend here didn't wait until tomorrow to get in trouble with the cops."

"It wasn't my fault!" Escalante protested.

"It surely was," Shana snapped. "Now, you make yourself useful when you leave here with … Jacob, is that right?"

Reuben sighed, hesitated for a moment, then said, "My name is Reuben Bane."

Escalante gasped, but the armorer simply smiled. "Thank you for being honest. No one will hear that name from me."

"You knew?"

"I guessed. Can't think of many civvies who'd have a 1911 unless they'd been excisers once. And if they'd retired and kept their weapon, they'd hardly be sneaking into Chattanooga, would they?

"Heard tell of a renegade exciser who's being hunted by the Foundation. Glad to see you've gotten away from them so far."

Reuben ran his hand over his forehead. Suddenly he felt exhausted. "I have a mission I must complete in West Virginia."

"Poacher who's become a gamekeeper?"

"Something like that."

"You hoping to put right what you did when you were an exciser?"

Reuben shook his head. "Nothing I do now can achieve that. It's a question of an ounce of credit to set against a ton of evil. But it is better than nothing."

She nodded, turned away and began putting together his supplies.

Chapter 18

TRASHTOWN

REUBEN LED LUCIFER ACROSS the remains of the railroad, threading his way between slumped and rusty shells and toward what had been the city recycling center before such things stopped mattering.

Now it was where all the garbage went that didn't get cast into the Tennessee River - or the Trickle as it was now widely known.

The horse flinched as the first hint of the coming stench reached his nostrils but, at a word from Reuben, he steadied himself stoically. Reuben hadn't spent long with the Rogens when he'd returned for Lucifer. The police had long gone, but the last thing the family needed was to attract any more attention to themselves.

He'd shared a word with Adam, then a hug from Lily, before heading into the darkness, having agreed to meet Escalante at the underpass that formed the boundary of the garbage tip. The merchant had headed off to find his mule which had drifted away from where he'd left it before being caught by the cop.

Reuben hoped Escalante hadn't been able to find the animal and had missed their rendezvous, but there he was, like the proverbial bad penny, waving at Reuben with obvious relief.

They were now passing into the garbage dump, and it was immediately obvious why the authorities didn't bother with any kind of wall or guards here. No one would willingly cross this cesspit and any larger force that tried it would be immediately bogged down and spotted long before they could mount a stealth attack.

Reuben kept his Navy revolver in its holster at his hip. It contained the last six rounds of the old ammunition, so he'd have six shots before needing to spend time reloading.

For his part, Escalante had a long rifle of inferior, modern make. It was a one-shot, muzzle-loaded smooth bore weapon that would only worry the ignorant. Good for scaring off coyotes, perhaps, but unlikely to be of any help in a real fight, especially in the close confines of the garbage dump.

"Stinks, doesn't it?" Escalante said. He was walking a pace behind the former exciser, presumably using Reuben as a partial shield.

"Why do you feel the need to state the obvious, Escalante?"

"Sorry, I guess I'm nervous. Call me Howie, will you?"

Reuben grunted. "Everyone calls you Escalante."

"Everyone called you Jacob."

"Touché. Now, which direction should we head in?"

The sun was rising in front of them, though it was hidden behind a vaporous cloud that might have been entirely generated by the trash heap, which reared up, a brown mound polluted by scraps of trash that poked through the surface. Here and there, especially around the lower slopes, grass grew as if the Earth were trying to cover over the blemish and swallow it. But, higher up, fresh garbage had been piled, brought to that level by a rickety scaffold and conveyor belt that Reuben imagined must be powered by animals.

At this time in the morning, however, the place was deserted except for tiny figures on the summit sifting through the trash for the scraps they lived on.

"We should keep off the mound," Howie said, gesturing to the left. "Follow the base around and we'll get a long way before we have to climb."

"I won't get Lucifer up there," he said.

"The only other option is to cross the river at the ford. But they'll be watching it."

Reuben didn't care. As they'd gone forward, the stench had risen so that he wanted to vomit every time he opened his mouth. Give him a full armed posse waiting at the ford's edge rather than this torture. His hand went to the wound on his arm. No, *that* had been torture. But at least the man who'd done it had paid with his life.

His eyes began watering as they made their way around the base, navigating between it and another, smaller mound, as if it were a river wending through a valley of filth.

Reuben's hands brought the revolver up as he saw movement from the left. Something was sifting through the soft crust of garbage to their left. More than one — dozens. At first, he thought they were animals. Some kind of monkey or ape that moved, bow-backed, periodically pushing a hand through the surface as if searching for hidden gold.

No, they weren't animals. It was as if his mind veered to the absurd rather than see what was actually there. They were apes – human apes. Many of them children and, as he and Howie approached, they noticed him and, one by one, vanished. Some ran, some buried themselves in the trash.

"Don't move, stranger."

Reuben spun around, searching for the voice.

"I said, don't move."

It was a man, dressed in black, gray and white camouflage and a black mask that, together, rendered him invisible against the garbage. At least, invisible to the distracted eye.

Beside him, two other figures resolved as they moved. They'd been standing in the shadow of the nearest mound as the sun rose behind it. Reuben cursed his stupidity and lack of attention. Maybe the stench had dulled his senses.

Howie stood to one side, hands in the air, using his mule as a shield. "Don't shoot, please! We're just passing through."

"No one just passes through," the man said. His accent was odd with a hint of Russian about it. "Not without our permission. Not without paying a toll."

Reuben sighed inwardly. Shana had given him some of his bits back as she hadn't had time to make his full order, but they would hardly be enough to satisfy a bandit.

"We'll pay!" Howie said. "How much?"

The bandit leader moved forward, and Reuben could see that he was a well-built Caucasian man in spotless fatigues. A beard emerged from around the black mask, and he wore mirrored sunglasses that had surely been plucked from the garbage. Deep down, in all likelihood, in the layers put there before the end of the world. No one would throw away such valuable items today, even if they had the effect of making the wearer look like a wasp.

"We don't need money, nowhere to spend it," the man said, coming closer. "We need food."

"You can have what we have," Ruben said, grinding his teeth at the thought of having to give up what the Rogens had given him but, nevertheless, reaching into his saddlebag.

The man shook his head and, as he did so, Reuben noticed more people emerging, some of them seemingly from within the garbage heap itself. There were at least a couple of dozen that he could see, with more movement beyond them.

"We will have that," the leader said, a smile spreading across his face. "And then we will have him."

He pointed first at Howie's mule, and then at Lucifer.

"We are very hungry, and fresh meat is hard to come by."

The leader's eyes met those of Reuben and the former exciser understood their meaning. Once the animals had been consumed, he and Howie would be next.

The revolver came up and the leader disappeared behind a cloud of black smoke. Reuben clambered onto Lucifer's back and shot into the mass of people. "No one kills my horse!" he shouted.

He looked down at Howie, who was already sitting on his mule. A spear flashed past Reuben's nose, and the air was full of black smoke as he returned fire, the stench of gunpowder momentarily overriding the stink of the garbage.

Lucifer surged toward Howie as the crowd, momentarily stunned, began closing in on them. He put his hand down. "Here, grab me!"

"No! I won't leave Myrtle to be eaten by them!"

"Then fight!"

With a feral cry, camouflaged figures reached down and began hurling anything they could find at Reuben, Howie and the animals.

Reuben targeted the closest and fired, then again. He reached down and grabbed the mule's reins and then nudged Lucifer on, speaking urgent, soothing words in the horse's ears as the big gelding hesitated.

They began edging forward, and Reuben felt hands grabbing his leg, so he pulled the knife from his belt and stabbed downward. The thing at his knee screamed and fell away.

He urged Lucifer forward, and they began to break free of the clutching hands. He turned to see Howie behind him, fighting off the grasping crowd of clawing creatures until, with a spurt, the mule accelerated, coming alongside Lucifer.

Then, just as he began to look ahead, believing they'd make it, he felt Lucifer's back drop a little as a weight landed and, simultaneously, the piercing heat of a stabbing stroke.

He felt hot breath on his neck, and he roared in pain as he wriggled in the saddle to get round, his enemy's teeth penetrating his shoulder. The creature roared, reared up, and he sensed something above him, a knife ready to sweep down.

Then a thunderous bang and the weight disappeared.

"Go!" Howie called out, striking left and right with the butt of his long rifle as the mule accelerated past Lucifer.

Reuben urged his gelding on and turned in the saddle to see a mass of people running toward them, a screaming, chaotic crowd straight out of the after days. After the fall of humanity.

He raised his revolver. How many rounds remained? Two? No more, certainly.

He lowered it, leaned down and grabbed the mule's bridle, using Lucifer's strength to encourage the beast to be quicker.

He ignored the warmth running down his back as, finally, they crested the hill and began accelerating toward the stream at the bottom and the ford across. A feral yell rent the air and one final missile fizzed past Reuben's head, and then they were away.

Chapter 19

REUNION

REUBEN OPENED HIS EYES and looked into the buck-toothed face of Howie Escalante.

"You okay, Rube? Thought I'd lost you for a minute."

"Where?"

"Not sure what this place is called, but it's the other side of the river, and I figure we're safe enough."

Reuben put his hand to his arm, then winced with pain as he found the wound.

"I fixed you up best I could. I know a little bush medicine. Say, what happened to your wrist?"

Reuben ran his fingers down from the fresh wound at the tip of his shoulder to the bandage on the inside of his wrist where the skin had been peeled away by the now dead Exciser Keller. It felt stiff and uneven beneath the bandage, but the pain had become little more than an itchy ache.

Howie said, "Look, I won't tell anyone. I owe you my life. If you hadn't kept them away, they'd be feasting on roasted Myrtle followed by a side serving of Escalante right now."

Reuben raised himself on his elbows, looking around desperately until he saw Lucifer standing outside.

They were in the ruins of a ranch house. Its windows had vanished at some point over the past decades and a fresh breeze soothed his face. "What happened? I remember crossing the ford, but then …"

"I figured you'd lost a lot of blood, but maybe you were just exhausted. Or it was the stench. Anyway, I grabbed your horse's reins and found this place."

"How far from the ford?"

"A mile or so. We'll have to get moving again before dark."

Pushing himself back against the wall, he used it to help lever himself to his feet. For a moment, he felt woozy, but then steadied himself and looked through the door, to what had been the backyard of the house. The rusting remains of a swing had become choked with climbing weeds, and would soon crumble into the ground. But everything seemed quiet with no signs of the cannibalistic horde they'd escaped from. And the air was clean, though the same couldn't be said for his clothes.

"Let's go," Reuben said.

"You sure?"

"We've got to move. There's only a strip of water between us and those demons." He headed to where Lucifer stood patiently, and gave the horse a handful of grain before checking him over. They'd been lucky. The gelding had many marks on his flanks, but nothing had penetrated his tough hide. Reuben felt the back of his own neck, finding teeth marks there but only dried blood. Lucky.

"By the way, thanks," he said as Howie busied himself preparing Myrtle.

"Least I could do. It was me who'd gotten us into the situation, after all."

"It was."

"So, what do we do now? You said you had friends outside the city."

"Yes, we'd better go find them," Reuben said, suddenly feeling anxious to find Skeeter and Asha. The young boy especially preyed on his mind.

He led Lucifer out of the backyard and onto the track outside then climbed wearily into the saddle.

"WHO'S THIS FELLA?" SKEETER gestured at Escalante as he led Myrtle up the slope toward the camp where Reuben had left them.

"His name's Howie. He helped me get out of the city."

"He comin' with us?"

Reuben shrugged. "That's up to him."

"Oh, I'll be coming, for sure," Howie said as he arrived, shaking hands enthusiastically with Skeeter. "You're heading north and east, you say? Plenty of opportunities."

"Where's Asha?" Reuben said.

Skeeter gestured behind him. "He's up at the overlook. We've been keeping a watch ever since you went. He's awful wound up. This morning, he woke up and ran up the hill. Said he had a bad feeling you were in trouble."

"Well, he wasn't wrong there," Reuben said.

Then the boy appeared running down the slope with his arms wide, crying out for joy.

And Reuben Bane, former exciser, got onto his knees and hugged the boy, relief coursing through his soul.

"ODD KID, THAT," HOWIE said, gesturing at Asha.

He and Reuben were sitting around the campfire while Skeeter warmed up a concoction made from the supplies Lily Dillard had given Reuben. Asha lay beside the fire, fast asleep. The first sleep he'd had since Reuben had left them to go into Chattanooga, according to Skeeter.

"I mean, he's small and half starved, but I reckon he's older than he looks. There's something about him."

Reuben grunted in agreement. He was wearing his backup pants as the ones he'd worn to Chattanooga were drying on an old brick wall at the top of the hill. He'd washed them in the travel cauldron, one piece at a time, and then taken them down to the foot of the hill to rinse them in a small stream, but he couldn't imagine he'd be able to get the stench of the garbage dump out of them entirely. Thirty-five years ago, he'd have thrown the lot in the trash without a second thought. The pants were those he'd worn when he'd ridden West with Marianna and Elinor hoping to be free of the Foundation. Well, his wife and daughter were indeed free, the plague had seen to that. Be careful what you wish for, Reuben thought.

"He's a deviant," Reuben said.

Howie gasped as Bane watched his reaction carefully. "He is? Feet?"

"Webbed toes."

Howie shrugged.

"It doesn't bother you?" Reuben asked.

"Why would it? Some of my best customers have been muteys." He put his hand to his mouth. "Am I allowed to say that word?"

Reuben smiled. "Not around the kid, though I don't imagine he'd take offence. You're right though, he's a strange child. And not because of his feet."

"He's not the only strange one," Howie said, nodding in Skeeter's direction.

Reuben smiled. "Yeah, I seem to draw them to me," he said, looking directly into Howie's eyes.

"Me? I'm straight as an arrow. Just a man trying to make an honest living."

"Two lies in one. But it's okay. You took out the thing that was taking a bite out of my neck."

Howie leaned forward and stretched out his hand. Reuben took it and, for a moment, felt as though he was seeing behind the mask. Howie Escalante was a hustler, that was for sure, but there was more to him than that. His persona was, to some extent at least, a shield that kept the world at bay.

"I'll make myself useful, you see if I don't," Howie said. "In fact ..."

He moved over to where Skeeter sat at the cauldron and took over.

The young man checked on Asha before coming to sit beside Reuben.

"Anything happen while I was in the city?"

Skeeter grunted, pointing over to where the boy lay. "He wouldn't go nowhere or do nothing until you came back. We've been no more than a couple of hundred feet of this spot for two days."

"And you saw nothing?"

"Oh, sure. Some folks heading the same way as you, some moving along the highway. Then we got surprised by a bear."

"You what?"

Chuckling, Skeeter looked over to where Howie was stirring the pot. "Just a black bear. Little one. But it came toward the fire, bold as you like. Didn't pay no heed to me, mind, even though I was the one pointing the gun. Sidled over to Asha and licked his face if you'll believe it!"

"What did the boy do?"

"He laughed. Seemed to know it didn't mean no harm. Gave it one of Mrs. Drew's dry apples and it disappeared. We never saw it again. But look, boss, are you sure about him?" He tilted his head in Howie's direction.

Reuben followed his gaze. "As sure as I am about any of you."

"Okay, boss. I guess you're in the business of seeing through folks who try to fool you."

Grunting Reuben said, "That was a former life, but I guess I know how *not* to judge people now."

"I think it's done," Howie said from the campfire.

"Smells great," Skeeter said.

And it did. Wafting across the little campsite was the aroma of Cajun cooking. It was as out of place as a spaceship descending from the heavens, and even woke Asha up.

"That doesn't smell like Mrs. Rogan's cooking," Reuben said.

"Oh, it was good enough, for sure, but I have some spices to give it an extra kick. They'd better, I've just put two bits' worth in there."

Reuben went over to sit with Asha as Howie handed out the bowls. Angel Drew had equipped them with enough crockery and cutlery for the three of them, so Howie waited with apparent patience while Asha finished his.

It was, indeed, the finest meal Reuben had eaten in what seemed like years. A simple vegetable stew had been elevated to the food of kings by Howie's spices.

He could have eaten more, but the cauldron was soon empty. If he'd had any bread, Reuben would have wiped the inside of the cauldron with it and damn what anyone thought of him.

\#

"So, where to tomorrow?" Howie said as he and Reuben were tending their animals.

"Knoxville," Reuben said. "After what I learned from the Rogens about what's going on in the West, I want to get my mission done as soon as possible."

"You have to find someone, I think?"

"A former scientist called Hannah Myers."

"Why is she so important that you were sent across the entire continent?"

Reuben's brush stopped moving as he looked over Lucifer's back. "That, my new friend, is an excellent question. This woman came from New Haven, and I guess the mayor wants her back."

"How long's she been gone?"

"Twenty years, I think."

Howie's eyebrows gathered together in the middle as he processed this.

"And she's the mayor's ex-wife," Reuben said. "So, maybe this is nothing more than a personal mission on his behalf. I didn't think I cared that much, to be honest. I owed the mayor and the town, and I thought it'd give me something to focus on while I decided what to do with the rest of my life."

"But?"

"But the more I see of the country outside of New Haven, the more I hope that she really does have some answers to make the world a better place."

Howie shrugged. "What do you mean? What have you seen?"

"Decay," Reuben said. "If we don't do something, and quick, it'll be the end of humanity."

Chapter 20

IDA

"HEY, SUGAR."

Hannah almost fell off her chair in surprise. "Ida, what are you doing here? You're supposed to be shut up in city hall, aren't you?"

"Seems to me this is the safest place to be right now. You're the only person I can be sure hasn't got it, except for the ones who've recovered, and they ain't exactly good company." The portly, gray-haired woman stood at the door of the kitchen, hands resting on the oak door frame. "My, you look like death warmed up. You gettin' any sleep?"

Hannah grunted. "Firstly, thanks, I know I look awful. And second, it comes with having a near death experience."

"Feelin' a little cranky, too, it seems. But, anyways, I didn't come here to give you earache."

"I know why you came, Ida."

Ida Beale shook her head and went over to the sink. "Well, it wasn't to wash up for you, that's for sure. But while I'm here ... "

Hannah settled back to her work, drawing off tiny samples of the test solution and dripping it onto petri-dishes. She'd isolated Roberto's granulocytes from what remained of the sample she'd recklessly injected into herself, and was attempting to culture them so she could use them to treat others.

She was focusing so closely, and was so exhausted, she didn't notice the mug of black until it appeared under her nose.

"Thanks."

"Why don't you take a break? Just for a moment. Indulge your friend. That's me, by the way."

Hannah looked up and smiled, feeling as though she were exercising facial muscles that had begun to atrophy from lack of use.

She got out of the wooden chair, only now realizing how sore her back — and backside — were.

"Gettin' old's a bummer, that's for sure," Ida said sympathetically. "But it beats the alternative."

Wordlessly, Hannah followed her friend into the cool dark of the sitting room, wincing as Ida threw the drapes wide and light flooded the room.

"That's better. Too much of your own company in a dark house drives you crazy at the best of times, and these ain't exactly them."

Hannah forced her shoulders to relax, feeling the tension ebb out of her body. Boy, she could do with some sleep. She sipped at her black, then looked across at her friend who was sitting on the moth-eaten sofa. "How's Mitch doing? And Lois?"

"There's my girl," Ida said. "Well, Mitch is hanging on in there. Mind he must be sick because he ain't interferin' with my runnin' of the council. There's just me and Emilio right now."

Hannah shook her head. "But he's not getting worse?"

"No. And he ain't gettin' better."

She was no epidemiologist, but Hannah hadn't heard of a virus like this before. Some people, it would kill within twenty-four hours. Others, it would bring low but, somehow, not kill them, at least not quickly. Toni Craft, for example. She was one of the first to come down with it and, last Hannah had heard, she was still alive.

If she was apt to entertain conspiracy theories, she might suspect the Foundation was behind this. Weaken the people so they welcome you with open arms when you offer help. But they'd been the first to be affected.

"And Lois?"

Ida shook her head. "She's taken it bad. Must have gotten a hell of an exposure. I don't reckon she's gonna make it."

"We can't lose her!"

"It's sad, for sure, but she ain't the only doctor in Mecklen."

"She's the only good one." Hannah settled back in her chair and took another shot of caffeine. It wasn't true, in all likelihood. At the last census, a little over two thousand people lived in and around the city. Statistically, that would include at least some who were medically competent, perhaps even one who'd been a doctor when the apocalypse had come. But Lois was special, Hannah was sure of it. She'd fought against her age, gender, appearance and size and yet was at least as competent as the best doctors from before the fall — in those areas of medicine that mattered most now, anyway.

"I reckon I've got enough cultured for two doses."

"She won't take it."

"I won't give her the choice."

Ida shook her head. "Seems to me you're fixin' on playing God. Or maybe you're more like Mitch than you'd like to admit."

"Maybe you're right. We haven't got enough doses for all that need meds, so how do we decide who we help? Lottery?"

"That'd be fairer, that's for sure."

"That doesn't make it the right thing to do. Lois is an asset to the city. Without her, more people will die, either from this plague or the next one."

Ida expelled a long breath, suddenly looking as exhausted as Hannah felt. "I don't know, but seems to me if we get to decide the value of human lives, that's a slippery slope, right there."

Getting to her feet, Hannah helped her friend up. "I get it. But I can't let Lois die, if I can do anything to stop it."

"Well, I ain't gonna do nothin' to get in your way." The old woman swayed, and Hannah put out a hand to steady her. "Don't worry none, I ain't got the plague. Had a fearsome earache and it's on account of Lois's antibiotics that I'm gettin' over it."

A thought hit Hannah between the eyes, and she almost didn't dare ask the clarifying question. "How's Toni Craft?"

"What? Oh, well she ain't dead. Should be, by rights. Mind, I haven't checked in on her since yesterday. What is it? What are you thinking?"

Hannah had her hand to her mouth, all exhaustion banished. "I wonder. Toni was given antibiotics, and she's still alive. You had antibiotics and you haven't caught it at all."

"Figured it was my Tennessee blood. But anyway, you said antibiotics wouldn't work on account of it being a virus."

By this time, Hannah had marched into the kitchen and was checking the vial of anti-viral she'd isolated. "It is a virus, I'm sure of it. But it's always been the case that different people get hit differently by any plague. Some folks get snuffed out as soon as the disease hits town, some die more slowly, some get sick and recover. And some people it passes right on by."

"You're sayin' I'm immune because I had antibiotics last week?"

"No, I'm saying it's more complicated than that."

"Ain't it always?"

Hannah swung round. "Look, it's like this. If we had enough of this treatment to go around," she said, pointing at the vial, "then we'd give it to everyone who got sick and it'd work for more or less all of them, and Bob's your uncle."

"Who's this Bob and what's he got to do with it? I ain't got a clue what you're talking about."

"Doesn't matter. The fact is, we *don't* have enough to go around, and I haven't figured out a way to make it quickly. I mean, we haven't got enough antibiotics, either. But maybe enough to give to the sickest people."

"But it won't cure them, will it?"

"It'll keep some of them alive, just like with Toni, until I can get enough of my treatment made."

Ida nodded. "I get you. So, what's next? Folks are dying right now, Hannah."

"I know. We need to ramp up the production of antibiotics and I have to work on making my granulocyte treatment much quicker. If we don't, the plague will get ahead of us and there'll be nothing I can do."

"It's got to be worth a shot. What do we do first?"

Hannah held up a small vial. "We give this to Lois. She's the only one who knows her process for antibiotics, and she's the only one who can help me with the antiviral."

"And if she don't agree?"

"She doesn't have a choice. Everything depends on her."

Chapter 21

O'Brien

ZAK STOOD BEHIND FATHER Ruiz as the last of the Shepherds took his seat in the council chamber. It was Father O'Brien, of course, and he shot a poisoned glance in Zak's direction before glaring at Ruiz who made no sign he'd even noticed.

Gripping his pad, Zak kept his gaze on Ruiz's right hand and tried to ignore the ache in his shoulder. If the priest wanted something recorded, he would flip his hand and Zak would write down the last thing spoken. This meant that he was expected to not only watch for the signal, but also to keep everything said in a kind of buffer memory in case it had to be written down.

Here, in this room containing nine men who could have him executed with nothing more than a signal to the guards, he stood, trembling, feeling utterly wretched.

Barber had been correct that Ruiz would be angry at Zak. It wasn't fair, of course. Zak had wanted to protest that their religion preached forgiveness but, in truth, he'd seen little evidence of that in his short life. And he wasn't completely stupid.

In fact, Ruiz hadn't made him suffer as much as Zak had expected. If anything, the priest seemed more nervous than angry, as if he were frightened of something. What could one of the nine most powerful men in the Foundation — in the former United States in fact — fear?

Only another shepherd, surely? As a lowly servant, Zak had no idea what plotting was going on at Foundation headquarters, just that something *was* happening here.

"Welcome shepherds."

The voice of First Shepherd boomed, and the priests and clerics became instantly silent. First was the oldest man here though his voice had lost none of its potency. Zak had heard him speak from the balcony several times and felt intimidated to be sharing the same room as him, breathing the same air.

He watched the man closely, fascinated. The First Shepherd had no hair on his chin or head, and sat like a vulture on his throne, set slightly above the level of the others. Zak didn't have a clue what First had done before the apocalypse — he'd heard rumors that he'd been a low-level politician — but he now spoke with complete authority. He'd been first among equals for thirty years now and, over that time, the Foundation had come to dominate the east of the American continent.

"I call to order this special session of the governing council, the first such for many years. We have matters of vital importance to discuss and I remind all that nothing we say here is to pass beyond these walls on pain of death." His gaze swept the room like a lighthouse beam, stopping when he locked eyes with Zak, who felt like a bug pinned to a board.

"Who are you, boy, and what are you doing here?"

Zak's tongue stuck to the top of his mouth, but Father Ruiz rose ponderously to his feet and spoke for him. "He is my servant, First Shepherd. I wish him to learn the tasks of a clerk."

"This is most irregular. We have trained clerics you could use."

"Indeed, First. I beg that you will permit this indulgence."

The First Shepherd's eyes darted to Zak, holding the boy in his gaze. "You understand my warning that nothing we say here is to be repeated?"

"Y... Yes, my lord."

"On pain of the fire?"

"Yes, my lord."

The First Shepherd looked at Ruiz and gave a little shrug. "It is your prerogative to order your household as you wish. I hope the boy rewards you in turn for this favor." There was a malevolent glint in the old man's eyes that sent a shiver up Zak's spine.

"Thank you, First Shepherd."

With that, the shepherd completed his sweep of the room, leaving Zak more perplexed than ever as to why Ruiz had insisted on his being here. But he had no time to ponder it.

"Father O'Brien," the First Shepherd said, "you called this extraordinary meeting. Please proceed."

Zak watched as O'Brien rose out of his chair like an unfolding clothes airer. His lean, almost skeletal fingers grasped a sheaf of papers in one hand while he slid his armless spectacles down his nose with the other. He looked like an academician about to present a dry treatise but, as Jacob had discovered, he was, in truth, a vicious brute.

"My fellow shepherds," he said, his gaze passing from one to the other and lingering, perhaps for a moment, on Father Ruiz. "I apologize for the disruption to your day and hope that we can conclude quickly so you may return to the preparation of spiritual food.

"The matter I wish to speak of is one of the highest import. You will be aware of my previous intelligence concerning the activities of a reactionary group in the former Washington State."

Again, he looked around the room, receiving a chorus of nodding heads, though little obvious enthusiasm or interest.

"As I reported at the time, they seek to spread their influence across the West and are pushing south toward California."

He stood up, pausing again for effect as Zak glanced at Ruiz. He'd served his master for long enough to be able to tell how he was feeling even when standing behind him. And Father Ruiz was angry. In fact, he was barely controlling his rage.

"Now, some of you will say, as you did last time I brought this to the attention of the council, that it is of little consequence. It's three thousand miles from this place to Seattle. Let them build their petty kingdom and we will crush them in their turn, once the rebel state of Texas has been dealt with. Am I correct?"

This time there was silence in the council chamber. The men there — men of power, but power is relative — knew that a hammer was hovering above the room waiting to drop on he who stuck out his neck first.

"Father Ruiz," O'Brien said, suddenly jabbing a skeletal finger toward Zak's master. "What do you say?"

Zak watched the familiar fat head look up, creasing the skin on the back of his neck.

"This is not my area of expertise, Father. I bow to your greater knowledge in this matter."

A thin smile spread across O'Brien's face. A game was being played here and, yet again, Zak didn't have a clue what the rules might be, or even what winning looked like.

"A humble reply from a humble shepherd," he said. "But we no longer have the luxury of turning a blind eye to matters in the West because, my friends, those matters are now having consequences in territories that are under our benevolent control."

He bent to his desk and picked up a sheet of paper which he glanced at before straightening again. "We must act on firm, firsthand intelligence, so I beg the First Shepherd's indulgence and request that we admit a trusted witness."

Zak could see that the First Shepherd was not surprised, but feigned curiosity. "This is irregular, Father O'Brien."

"These are irregular times, honored shepherd. I do not apologize since I believe the testimony provided will eliminate much unnecessary debate."

"Bring forward your witness."

O'Brien nodded his thanks, then pointed to a guard at the door who went out, returning followed by a compact man similar enough to O'Brien that he could have been hatched from the same clutch if it weren't for the fact that he looked a decade or so younger.

"This is Representative Carver," O'Brien said. "He has come from the city of Mecklen which recently accepted our protection."

A gasp went up in the chamber, but it was Ruiz who gave voice to the shock. "The plague town? He has come from there? Are you insane?"

O'Brien's face tightened momentarily, but he made a dismissive motion, directing his attention solely to Ruiz. "You think me such a fool? Carver has been quarantined. He is not infected."

"Shepherds!" First Shepherd said, his voice rising above the clamor. "This is a place of civility. I will not tolerate such disrespect. Father Ruiz, you are one of the most senior among us, I expect more from you."

Zak saw the back of Ruiz's neck flush red and he sat back down. "I apologize," he said, forcing the words out. "This chamber contains the combined wisdom of decades. If pestilence were to strike among us, who would guide our flocks?"

O'Brien's hooded eyes glinted. "You are forgiven, my friend. Your concern for us all only serves to remind us of your kindness. But please be reassured that Representative Carver poses no threat to this council, he is here merely to report."

"Then proceed," First Shepherd intoned.

Carver emerged nervously from where he'd stood while the shepherds debated to stand facing their long table, addressing himself to First Shepherd.

"My name is John Carver and it is my honor to be a representative of the blessed Foundation and my privilege to assist in the task of bringing more of the unguided into the embrace of our faith."

"You are welcome, Carver," First said. "Yours is surely the work of God for it not only spreads enlightenment but also aids the purification of the gene pool."

Carver bowed. "I thank you, my lord."

"Proceed with your report," O'Brien said, and Zak wondered at his interruption. Perhaps he was also nervous.

Zak listened closely, making notes when indicated by Father Ruiz, as Carver recounted his mission to Mecklen, and he sensed impatience in Ruiz and others there as there was, so far, no reason why this report couldn't have been read out by a cleric as was normal. Why was Carver here?

O'Brien raised his hand, clearly wishing to take back control. "Representative, that is interesting and commendable, but time is precious and what you have told us so far is merely the window dressing."

"Forgive me, holy shepherds," Carver said, flushing bright red. "All was going to plan when the plague arrived. The first victim was my protector, Branch. He had recently returned from a covert mission into the West."

"So, he brought the plague back with him?" Ruiz asked.

"Yes, my lord."

"And what of that? If our enemies succumb to pestilence that is a good thing, surely?"

O'Brien leaned forward and looked directly at Ruiz. "If it were only to kill our enemies, then I would agree with you. But this is not just any plague, it is a weapon created by the enemy in Washington State and used against the people of the West to bring it under their control. And now, my friends, that weapon is being unleashed on us and we have no defense."

Silence blanketed the room as O'Brien looked around, unable to completely hide his delight.

Out of the corner of his eye, Zak saw Ruiz frantically scribbling while shielding his hands from those around him.

"My fellow shepherds, I regret to inform you that the first cases of pestilence have been discovered in New Boston. We are, therefore, in a state of war."

Ruiz reached around and grabbed for Zak's arm, pulling him down.

O'Brien didn't notice. He was directing all his attention to First Shepherd.

"Find Barber and give him this. Then follow his instructions," Ruiz hissed in Zak's ear.

"But Father..."

"Do it! Her life depends on it!"

"Who...?"

But he knew who Ruiz meant. The only person whose life the priest valued more than his own.

"Go! You will get a chance to slip away in a moment."

Then the pressure on Zak's arm disappeared and he stood again.

O'Brien now looked around the council chamber. "We must have strong leadership now to save us all. There is no time for debate, so I invoke the emergency ordinances and call for a vote."

There was uproar as shepherds and their clerics got to their feet and all began talking at once. Zak turned to see the doors opening and guards coming into the chamber.

Finally, he understood. This was a coup. A play for power. Absolute power. And, in their terror, the shepherds would appoint O'Brien.

Ruiz turned to him and waved him toward the door. "Go!" he said over the chaos. "Save her."

And he knew what Ruiz meant. O'Brien would make Eve his and, as Zak thought of Jacob's injuries, caused by the masochistic priest's violence, he knew what he had to do. Somehow, he had to rescue Eve or see her suffer the same fate.

Chapter 22

KNOXVILLE

REUBEN DROVE LUCIFER TOWARD the small settlement nestling on the side of a hill just south of Knoxville. It had been Asha who'd noticed the patch on Reuben's arm glowing as they passed into the shade of a tree. He'd left the others behind to follow as he searched for somewhere for them to shelter.

Two men emerged from the side of the road, rifles pointing at the former exciser as he brought the horse to a halt.

"Hold it!" A third man walked into the center of the road, hand raised in warning. "Folks who ride like the Devil himself is on their tail are apt to get knocked off their horse. This is border country, and we don't welcome strangers."

Reuben reined in Lucifer, holding him still as the horse snorted as if he were offended at the man's impertinence. "My name is Jacob Day," he said, keeping his voice calm and authoritative. "Has no one sounded the alarm?"

"Alarm? Why?"

"You don't have a Geiger counter?"

The man, who wore a pair of spectacles that were missing one arm, looked up to the sky. "I don't see nothing."

Reuben couldn't hide the exasperation in his voice. He pulled a patch of cloth from his pocket and held it high before cradling it in his palm. "Come closer."

"Do I look stupid?"

Resisting the severe temptation to answer in the affirmative, Reuben instead leaned down and handed the patch to the man. "Here, see for yourself."

One of the other guards huddled next to the leader and leaned in. "Well, I'll be... Linus, get yourself over to the church and ring the bell. And be quick!"

The leader squinted up at Reuben, regarded him for a moment, then put his hand up.

"Name's Rufus Cain. Thanks, stranger. You'll be needing shelter until the storm passes, I reckon."

"I'd appreciate that. Three friends of mine are following, they will also need a place to hide."

Cain's eyes narrowed. "Fellas like you?"

"Not exactly. One's riding a mule, another a pony. That's why I've gone ahead."

Smiling, Cain said, "Then we'll wait awhile, and all go in together."

IT TOOK ONLY FIVE minutes or so for the others to appear in the distance. "Well, that's the weirdest band of brigands I've ever seen, I reckon."

Despite knowing that the sky above the clouds was riddled with radiation, Reuben couldn't help but laugh as Howie appeared on the back of his mule, with Skeeter on his full-size horse on the other side of Asha, making a perfect incline from left to right.

"Come now," Cain said, encouraging them on. "I reckon I can feel my brains boiling."

He led them past a sign that declared this to be Sevierville to a small church that stood in the center of the cluster of homes, its bell tolling the warning. They joined a short line of people waiting to get inside, all with sleeping rolls and overnight bags.

"Hey, Pastor," Cain said, shaking the hand of the priest standing at the door, ushering people inside.

The priest was remarkably tall but, unlike Skeeter, he was perfectly proportioned. He looked like someone had inflated him like a tire.

"Welcome, strangers, I am Father Cheng," he said, his voice deep and resonant. "Come inside and shelter from the storm."

Reuben took the man's outstretched hands, sensing the remarkable strength within, but the priest only held him for a moment before moving onto the others.

"Why do people come here?" Reuben asked Cain once they were inside, "Why not shelter at home?"

Cain smiled and pointed up. "The roof is lined with iron. It's the safest place to be."

Reuben looked up and then around the little church. "It's been built recently," he said. He'd seen many rebuilt churches and chapels, but rarely of this quality outside the cities or Foundation-dominated areas. This church was, to all appearances, exactly the kind of place that might have been built at any time in the past couple of centuries. A wooden structure with plain windows and varnished pews. The floor, by contrast, was of bricks embedded in the ground.

"Yeah, the pastor got us all together soon after he arrived here. Said we needed a place to come together, especially in dark times. We salvaged every scrap of iron and steel for miles around."

Reuben sensed the approach of the priest. "It's a huge Faraday cage."

"Indeed," Cheng said. "Though it functions more as a simple radiation shield since I'm not sure there's much technology left that would be vulnerable to an electromagnetic pulse."

Reuben thought about the e-book reader in his pack, feeling an almost irresistible desire to get it out and check it was adequately shielded. But he hadn't become a leading exciser without mastering his desires. "You're surely not old enough to have been alive when the lights came first?"

"I was a child," the priest said with a smile. He had a thick, black beard and no hint of the East Asian ancestry his name suggested. "My adoptive mother was an engineer. She survived the first waves, and imparted much of her wisdom to me before her death a few years later."

He rubbed at his chin, before laughing. "Yes, a country pastor is an unlikely occupation for the son of an engineer! But my mother spent her life trying to solve problems for people, and to help them. In this new world I am doing much the same in my own way. Now, who is this?"

Asha had appeared, quietly entering the church with Howie.

"Lucifer's fine," he said. "There's a barn over there, and all the animals are in there, now."

Having delivered his report, Asha then looked up at the priest in amazement.

Cheng kneeled so that his eyes were at the same level as the boy. "Welcome to my church. You are safe here."

"I know," Asha said.

"Why have you brought your saddlebags in?" Reuben asked, his attention on the little merchant who was struggling under their weight.

"No offence, but I'd rather keep my goods close to me."

Cheng smiled and shook his head. "They would be quite safe, my suspicious friend, but no matter. Now, why don't you have some food while we wait out the storm."

Skeeter took Asha by the hand and led him toward the back of the church where a trestle table had been set up. A line had formed and, behind the table, two people stood supervising a row of metal plates containing food of different forms.

Reuben went to follow Howie as he headed after the others, when Cheng pulled gently on his arm and leaned close, bending forward so he was at Reuben's head height.

"That boy, what's his story? How do you know him?"

Reuben was instantly suspicious. "Why do you want to know?"

"It is my responsibility to know at least something of those who shelter here. I owe that to my people."

"He was alone, so I took him under my protection. Why would you fear a boy?"

Cheng grubbed at his beard, glancing to where Asha and Skeeter had reached the head of the line. "I don't fear him, but there is something odd about him."

"What do you mean?"

"I don't know. I sense that there is more to him than meets the eye. He is like an iceberg. I think that what I see of him is just a fraction of what is there."

Reuben shrugged. "He's just a kid." It was a lie. Though he couldn't identify why, Asha was more than just a kid to Reuben. He'd put it down to his own guilt at a dark past persecuting people like Asha, but he had begun to wonder. There was *something* about him. And the priest, it seemed had picked up on it.

Realizing he wasn't going to get more from Reuben, Cheng said, "I'm sorry, please go eat."

By the time Reuben sat down to some food, the others had all finished. They were sitting in a circle in one corner of the church, and Reuben was enjoying a delicious oatcake with a hard local cheese while half listening to the people around them talking and laughing. There was a definite party atmosphere, or, at least, a feeling that this was routine and an opportunity for the community to get together.

Then he noticed that Asha, who was sitting next to him, was looking down at his empty plate, not moving.

"What is it? Are you still hungry?"

Asha started as if he'd been shocked out of a trance, then he looked up at Reuben. "No, I'm not hungry."

"So, what's eating you?"

"It's the tall man. The priest," he said, leaning in, his voice barely more than a whisper.

"What about him, he seems to me to be a good man. It's because of him that this church is here for us to shelter in."

"I think he is a good man. But," he said, checking around them and putting his hand against Reuben's ear to shield their conversation, "he's like me."

Chapter 23

CATLETTSBURG

THEY STAYED WITH RUFUS Cain and his wife that night, once the lights faded from the dark skies.

Reuben had questioned Asha after his revelation about the priest, but the boy wouldn't — or couldn't — say anything more. It seemed fanciful to imagine that Asha had a built-in mutant-detector, but perhaps he was able to pick up on some aspect of the man's behavior that gave him away. If that became known to the Foundation, Asha would suddenly turn from being their nemesis to their most valuable asset. A kind of deviant-hunter's canary.

Aside from his size, Pastor Cheng didn't seem to be anything other than normal but then Reuben knew only too well that the sorts of deviation that would sentence the bearer to death might be hard for any but an exciser to detect.

Reuben rubbed his injured shoulder as he made his way toward the church. Howie had been looking after it, rubbing his own brand of snake oil into the wound and, perhaps despite that rather than because of it, it was healing well. Cain walked with him, pointing at newly refurbished buildings with obvious pride.

He'd explained the previous night that most of the men in the area worked in the re-opened iron mine and were paid in a pseudo-currency called "Bread-scrip" that could only be spent in Knoxville and the surrounding area. Reuben detected the resentment in Cain's voice that they'd become dependent on the company store for their essential supplies, but the pastor had arrived, and the mood had changed. The community had focused its spare energy on building the church which had become the place they all looked to in times of doubt. And then to refurbishing their homes as each needed it.

Cheng had preached about the transient nature of all forms of money and, though he'd never openly supported the mining company's use of scrip, neither had he opposed it. He simply considered it unimportant.

Reuben was cynical enough to suspect an ulterior motive. Perhaps the company had put the priest here to keep the population satisfied with their situation though, frankly, it didn't seem to him that they had it too bad. Sevierville, to all appearances, was peaceful and, if not exactly prosperous, he detected no lack. The people here were adequately fed and without obvious fear. Maybe freedom was a price they'd pay for that. And he wouldn't blame them if that were the case.

"Ah, there you are," the priest said as he saw them approach. "Has my friend Rufus treated you well?"

Reuben glanced over at Cain. "He has. May fixed us a delicious breakfast this morning."

"She is an excellent cook," Cheng said with a broad smile. "You're a lucky man, Rufus."

"I am, that," Cain said, flushing. "Now, I have some chores to do. The next shift leaves in half an hour and I'm the driver."

Reuben shook his hand. "Thank you for your hospitality, Rufus. It has been refreshing to meet you and remind myself that there are still good people in this world."

As they watched the man go, the priest put his arm around Reuben's shoulder and guided him around the church building, smiling and waving to his congregation as he went.

"What are your plans?" he said as they walked. "You are, of course, welcome to stay with us to recover from your journey, though you will be expected to sing for your supper."

"Thank-you, but we'll move on today."

"You're certain?"

"We are. We have a long way to go."

The priest paused as they reached the corner of the white-painted church. "And the boy? He goes with you?"

"He does. He's in my care."

"He has an interest in your destination?"

Reuben tried to keep his temper under control, but his gratitude and good feelings toward the priest were evaporating. Probably because the man was gnawing away at Reuben's uncertainty about whether it truly was good for Asha to remain with him.

"He has an interest in being with me."

Cheng looked him in the eye and then nodded. "I understand. Have you planned your route?"

"It's essentially just north and east."

"You'll want to avoid what remains of the Douglas Reservoir. Get trapped on this side of it and you'll find yourself in a maze of swamps and mudflats. Your animals will never get through even if you do."

Reuben nodded. He had a route map from before the fall, and he'd seen the reservoir on it.

"My advice is to head directly north. You'll pass through what used to be a place called Catlettsburg, though it's a ghost town now. There's a bridge a few miles past that; takes you over the river. We keep that creek dredged, so you have to use the bridge. That'll take you past what was the reservoir and if you stay on the highway, you'll hit I-40 in the end. I wish you a safe journey."

"Any ambush points on the way?"

"Watch yourself in Catlettsburg. The ruins make for good cover, but once you're past them, you should be okay until I-40."

Reuben shook the pastor's massive hand. "Thank you."

"I hope you'll return if you journey this way, you owe us a day's labor!" he said with a brittle smile.

"I will."

Reuben turned on his heels and walked back toward Rufus Cain's house, wondering why a sense of unease had descended upon him.

EVENING WAS FALLING BY the time they reached the edge of Catlettsburg. Reuben had gone ahead with Skeeter while Howie and Asha stayed on the edge of the former town until signaled.

The pastor hadn't been exaggerating when he'd called Catlettsburg a ghost town. A robbed-out railroad track hemmed them in on the right, its warning signs bent, twisted and rusted.

To the left, they passed the shell of a rectangular building with what Reuben recognized as the Arby's logo, then a burned-out Goodwill followed by a Mc-Donald's that had become overwhelmed by trailing weeds, its famous arches looking like a drowning swimmer raising his arms in hope and fear.

"I don't see nothing," Skeeter said.

"Me neither. Give the signal."

Skeeter had been keeping the embers of a ciga-rette alight, and used them to kindle a makeshift rush torch that he held up.

Soon enough, as Reuben scanned the shadows with his 1911, Asha and Howie trotted up. He hadn't fired the weapon with Shana's new cartridges yet, so he'd loaded three rounds into the clip with the remaining six being his trusty original ammunition. That way, if they were attacked and the black pow-der rounds didn't work, he'd only have to shoot three times to return to his standard ACP. Assuming the new ammunition didn't jam the mechanism. And that he had time for three shots.

"It sure is creepy," Skeeter said as they resumed.

Though he wasn't about to admit it, Reuben agreed. There was something about the way the wind whistled along the valley that gave even him the shivers. He'd spent decades on the road, trav-eling to places that varied from those that were almost as civilized as before the fall to some that were a vision of what might come next if the de-cay wasn't stopped. Like the garbage dump outside Chattanooga. But he'd rarely come across anywhere as desolate as this. It was as if this landscape knew what it had lost and was in mourning.

He wished he'd asked the pastor what had happened here to lead to its abandonment. Sure, plenty of towns, villages and cities had been left to crumble, but Catlettsburg felt as though it had died more recently.

They followed the highway, with the abandoned railroad to their right, as the darkness deepened and the breeze picked up, rustling the leaves of the line of trees they could dimly make out running along a ridge to their left.

The ghostly spire of a white-painted chapel emerged from the darkness, standing in a weed-choked parking lot and illuminated by a half moon lurking behind the clouds.

Reuben had swung his 1911 around before he'd even become consciously aware of the movement. "Show yourselves!" he yelled, his voice echoing in the unnatural silence.

"You see something?" Skeeter asked, eyes scanning the shadows.

A figure emerged and walked confidently toward them. He wore a sheriff's uniform or, at least, a good facsimile, with a wide brimmed hat and a shining badge. He held a Remington 870 shotgun two handed and he purposefully pumped a shell into the chamber as he strode. Behind him, shapes moved so Reuben was in no doubt that they were hopelessly outnumbered.

"Lower your weapon, mister," the man said. "Name's Smallwood, and I'm the law here."

"Whose authority?"

"The mining company," he said, "and this."

He held the gun up, sighting directly at Reuben along the barrel.

"Oh, and them," he added as the other figures emerged into the diffuse moonlight.

Reuben counted a dozen or so, all on foot. Presumably, they'd tethered their horses behind the church.

"What do you want with us?" Reuben said.

Smallwood looked beyond Reuben, pointing at Asha. "Word is you got a mutey. Now, if you hand him over, peaceful like, then you can ride on your way. Make any trouble, and you'll all end up before the judge, not just the deviant."

Hot blood filled Reuben's mouth as he bit the inside of his cheek. That damned priest. Somehow, Asha's instinct had been shared by Cheng and he'd reported it to the local law enforcement. No wonder he'd wanted to delay them. Reuben couldn't imagine how they'd gotten here ahead of them given that there was only one highway out of Sevierville.

He gestured at Asha to move closer on Blossom.

"Hey, you hear me? Don't you start a fight you don't have a chance to win. There's no need for any blood to be shed."

"Except his?" Reuben said, pointing at Asha.

Smallwood shrugged. "That's for the judge to decide."

"Isn't it a matter for an exciser?"

"We don't have no truck with the Foundation," Smallwood said, though with obvious nervousness in his voice.

"Then why do you care about so-called muteys? You can see he's only got one head."

"It's not for me to decide. I got my orders."

"From Cheng?"

"From the chief."

Reuben could see from the man's reaction that, despite his words, the priest was behind this.

Smallwood continued, "Now, you gonna come or are things gonna get nasty."

"I'm going to give you one warning, Sheriff," Reuben said. "Let us pass and you and your men will leave this place on their feet. Stand in my way, and many will not return to their wives and children."

That certainly hit home, but Smallwood was now performing in front of his men, so he puffed himself up and jabbed his shotgun at Reuben. "You're threatening an officer of the law! That's a hanging offence right there."

"It's not a threat, it's a promise. I do not wish to harm you."

Smallwood was wavering, but then a large shape emerged from the shadows. "You are a weak man, Smallwood. I will see this through."

It was Pastor Cheng, though now he was dressed like the other deputies, in blue denims. He strode toward Reuben.

Beside him, two more men walked across the highway, Skeeter and Howie covering them with their weapons.

"Now, you see here!" Smallwood roared. "This is my operation, I'll handle it my own way!"

Cheng turned to the sheriff and pulled the shotgun from his grip and, while Reuben and the others were distracted, someone moved behind them.

"Boss! They got Asha!"

Reuben spun around to see Asha on the floor, the arms of a strong man around him, a knife at his throat. Howie was laying, arm's splayed, on the ground, out for the count.

Cheng stepped in and took the Colt from Reuben's unresisting hands.

"And that, Smallwood, is how you do it," Cheng said in his deep, confident voice. "Now, you will return to the town with us," he added to Reuben. "You will face quick justice, I'm sure. It's a pity you didn't yield when our weak sheriff gave you the opportunity, we could have concluded our business and you would be on your way by now. Sadly, Catlettsburg is going to remain the farthest you got on your journey east. You will remain here for a long time, I suggest. Or, if you're unlucky, a brief time."

"You're going to have us hung?"

"No, indeed. The boy will die, regrettably, so that his defect can be eliminated from the population, but you will work off your debt to the community in the iron mines."

Reuben treated Cheng to a baleful stare. "And what, preacher, of your defect? Or doesn't the chief know about it?"

He was fishing, but he knew immediately that he'd struck home.

"My size? Is that what you consider a defect? That is simply a gift from Our Lord to aid me in my ministry."

Reuben shook his head, aware that Smallwood and his men were watching. He lowered his voice, so only the priest could hear. "No, I'm talking of your secret. The secret you wanted to prevent Asha ever revealing. How pathetic you are, so-called man of God, to seek to murder a child so you can remain safe from being accused of the very same crime as him."

Bane didn't see the fist swing, he simply felt its impact and pitched sideways from the horse. He heard cries going up around even as the wind was knocked out of him when he hit the ground.

Strong hands lifted him, turning him around so he hung there, dazed, while the fist came at him again. Somehow, he managed to duck out of the way, before kicking the priest in the groin. The effect was almost entirely non-existent, Cheng just groaned a little, as if Reuben had kicked his leg, then swung his fist into Bane's stomach, propelling him backward with a grunt. He lay on the ground looking up at the dark sky, a few stars shining fitfully above. His brain felt as though it had been put through a blender, but he tried to lever himself up on his elbows.

A huge shape loomed above him, blocking out the stars and Wade was hauled to his feet again as Skeeter stood at bay, covered by one of the priest's men. Reuben hadn't seen him in the settlement and now knew that Cheng had his own private contacts within the Knoxville authorities.

"Let him go," the pastor said to the man holding Reuben, "but watch him. If he makes a move, shoot him."

A fourth man had hold of Asha, a big hand on the boy's frail shoulder. The knife had been withdrawn, but was still at the man's waist.

"Now then, Sheriff Smallwood, you may take the others into custody. I will take the boy."

Sheriff Smallwood stepped reluctantly forward, followed by three of his deputies.

"Pastor, are you sure? He seems like just a kid to me."

The voice came from the man holding Asha.

"He's trembling. Shouldn't we let the sheriff deal with it?"

Cheng thrust a finger in the man's direction. "How dare you, Askey? Who is the master of spiritual matters here?"

The man Askey looked away, shaking his head. "You are, Pastor, of course. I just wouldn't want this burden on your soul."

"How dare you?" Cheng roared. He stepped forward, leaning down to grab a howling Asha out of Askey's hands. For a moment, the wretched man looked as though he was going to protest, but then he simply turned around, looking away from the boy.

At that moment, a shot rang out and the pastor fell backward, clutching his arm and throwing Asha to the floor. Reuben brought his elbow up and caught the man behind him on the chin, then dropped, sitting across his chest and grabbing the 1911. He should have shot him there and then, but Skeeter had jumped on his captor, thin arms raining blows on the surprised man, so Reuben stood up, keeping the 1911 pointed at the man he'd stunned, then pressed the cold metal against the temple of Skeeter's opponent.

Throughout, Sheriff Smallwood hadn't moved. Neither had his men.

Reuben got to his feet, pulled Asha behind him as Howie covered Askey. He'd obviously been playing dead and had used his single shot rifle to fell the pastor. Whether Askey knew the weapon was now empty didn't matter much as the man had no inclination to move.

"I suggest you leave them to me, Sheriff," Reuben said as the stunned lawman took in the carnage.

"I was a mine supervisor until six months ago," he said. "Previous sheriff got himself arrested on trumped up charges and they pinned the badge on me."

"I'm sorry, but you need to understand the difference between the law and justice. A good lawman serves the latter. I learned that from the man who gave me this weapon."

At ground level, the priest moaned and clutched at his arm, cursing as he lay there.

Sheriff Smallwood gestured to him. "Talking of justice. What are you gonna do with him?"

"I haven't decided yet. I was in Sevierville, and he's done a lot of good. The people there wouldn't welcome me delivering him what he deserves. I wonder how many people he'd been responsible for persecuting to protect his own skin?"

Then an idea struck Reuben, and he pulled the sheriff closer. "I'm going to tell you something now, and leave it to you to decide what to do with the information. If I were you, I'd keep it as leverage. Tell one other — someone you trust — as security."

"What is it?"

"I wasn't bluffing. He's a deviant."

"What?"

"But remember, he's done much good. Should he be persecuted merely for an accident of birth?"

The sheriff rubbed his chin. "I've never been happy with it, myself. Seems to me most of the muteys I ever met were nothin' more than folks like me with some small difference that don't mean nothing."

"Then it's time to do something about it."

Reuben turned to the captured men. "You can go back. The sheriff will turn you free when you get to the city. As for you," he said, kneeling beside the groaning priest, before leaning close so only Cheng could hear, "The sheriff knows your secret. I'm going to let you live, assuming the wound doesn't kill you, but I will return. And if I find that you've abused your position in any way, then I will hunt you and I will blow your brains out. You won't know where I am or when it will happen, only that it *will* happen. Send no one after us. Report the boy dead if you must say anything. Do I make myself perfectly, crystal clear?"

The priest looked from Reuben to the sheriff. He formed a gob of spit in his mouth but, at the last moment, cast it into the dirt rather than at Reuben. He gave a tiny nod and Reuben watched as the sheriff corralled Cheng and his men and disappeared behind the church.

As Reuben and the others were preparing to resume their journey, an ancient Army truck emerged, turned on the highway and headed back the way they'd come. He wondered if the sheriff, or the city, knew just how priceless that piece of junk was now.

"Nice play acting, Howie," he said, slapping the little man on his shoulder. "And good shooting."

Howie smiled coyly. "I was aiming for his heart."

"I wish I'd'a thought of that," Skeeter said.

Reuben shook him by the hand. "You took your chance when it came, that's all I ask. Your brawling skills need a little improvement, that's all."

He turned to Asha, who was already on Blossom's back. "And what about that Jedi mind trick you played on the goon?"

Asha shook his head. "What's a Jedi?"

"Well, I'm beginning to think you are."

"I just thought he wasn't a bad man, that's all."

Reuben climbed into Lucifer's saddle. "You thought the same of Cheng. Keep your secret for now, but you're one hell of a weird kid, Asha."

He nudged the horse along the highway, trying to still his racing thoughts. The mystery of Asha was only getting deeper the more he knew the boy.

Chapter 24

Burden

Zak found Master Sergeant Barber in the weapons antechamber where he was polishing a practice sword.

"What is it, boy?" he said, dropping the sword as Zak tried to draw air into his lungs.

He'd run down three flights of stairs to get here, all the while trying to avoid being spotted. Who was he hiding from? He had no idea. He hoped the master sergeant would know what to do.

Zak held out the scrap of paper he'd been given by Ruiz and waited as the protector read it, his face hardening as he did so.

"Do you know what this says?"

Zak shook his head.

"Ruiz gave this to you personally?"

"I ... I was in the ... council chamber."

"And O'Brien has taken control?"

Zak tried to compose his thoughts. "No. Not before I left, anyway. Maybe somebody stood up to him, stopped it. Maybe the father."

"No, Ruiz doesn't have it in him, and O'Brien won't have stirred this up if he wasn't pretty certain of winning. Chances are most of the other shepherds were in his pocket before he made his move."

Barber stood, reading the paper and shaking his head. "The son of a bitch." He turned the last sheet and handed it to Zak.

"This is for you."

His hands shaking, Zak read these words in the unmistakably cramped handwriting of Father Ruiz.

"*Isaac. I place Eve's safety in your hands. Take her out of New Boston and protect her until I send word. Trust only those that Barber trusts. Farewell.*"

And, beneath the message, a hastily scrawled signature.

"Come on then," Barber said, grimly, leading Zak into his small office beside the main training area. He lifted down a leather scabbard that held a short sword and looped it through his belt. Then he opened a drawer and pulled out a black revolver. "It was my father's," he said. "And before that, his grandfather's. God knows there's no elegance to it, but it's effective and we're going to need all the help we can get."

Barber took a canvas bag and put the revolver inside followed by two boxes of rounds.

He opened another locked drawer. "Here, take this," he said, handing a bladed weapon in a small leather sheath to Zak.

"Th... thank you," he said.

"Listen, you understand what Ruiz is asking?" He bent down to look Zak in the eyes.

"Protect Eve?"

"Sure, but we'll be going up against the Foundation council. If Ruiz is right and O'Brien has seized control, we'll be traitors."

Zak gulped. "Okay."

"We'll never be able to come back, you get that?"

He hadn't, in truth, but still he nodded.

Barber gave a tiny grunt. "Son of a bitch. Twenty years I've served faithfully as a protector. All for nothing. My reputation burns with me. Come on. Let's hope Ruiz has delayed them."

"WHICH WAY?" BARBER SAID as they made their way through the corridors of the Foundation HQ. They'd moved as quickly as they could without attracting undue attention and, so far, there was no sign that anything out of the ordinary was happening.

But now they had a choice to make. The same choice Zak had faced when he'd escorted Eve. And he made the same decision. "The kitchens. Mr. Wong will help us."

He'd been surprised that the master sergeant had even asked him, and even more surprised that the big man simply nodded his agreement.

"I'll follow you."

Zak led the way down a level until they reached the kitchen. He breathed a sigh of relief when he saw the broad back of Wong at the counter.

"Ah, you're back. How's your shoulder?" he said, then he looked at the figure following Zak. "Master Sergeant, welcome to my kitchen."

To Zak's surprise, Barber stepped forward and shook hands with the chef. "It's good to see you."

"I wish I could say the same. I guess everything's going to shit up there?"

Barber nodded solemnly.

"Tearing themselves to pieces over the girl, I expect."

"No," Zak said, "plague has come, sent by some enemy. I don't really understand it."

Wong scratched his beard as he nodded. "And O'Brien is taking control of the council?"

"Yes," Barber said.

"Then it *is* about the girl."

"Father Ruiz wants us to take her out of the city," Zak said.

"I'm sure he does. My, that girl has a power, doesn't she? You've felt it, my boy, despite my warnings. But you can be forgiven of course, you're young enough to be a slave to your hormones. Those vultures in the council have no such excuse."

Barber said, "What do you suggest?"

"Do as Ruiz says. He may be a fat fool, but his motives are good, in this at least. She must be kept out of O'Brien's claws."

"Yes!" Zak said.

"Oh, not just for her sake, my boy, though surely that's a good enough reason for you to risk everything. But the master sergeant here? I'm not so sure he'd sacrifice his life for a girl he's never met."

Barber flushed, then nodded. "It's true."

"Then why? What's so important about her?" Zak asked.

"The clue's in the name they've given her. She is to be the mother of the pure. He who controls Eve controls the future."

THE GRAY-HAIRED SISTER GREER looked doubtfully at Wong, Barber and Zak when they were brought in front of her, but when Barber showed her the note Ruiz had scribbled, she relented and sent for Eve.

"So, it's come to this, has it? Ruiz was too late."

"What do you mean, Reverend Sister?" Barber asked.

"He knew this was coming, but he hoped to have secured Eve's future first. He is a good man, but he underestimates the cunning of Father O'Brien. Where will you take her?"

"I'm not sure. I lived in Plymouth and know the area, so perhaps there."

She opened her mouth to respond, and, at that moment, a distant bell began pealing.

"You must go!" Sister Greer said. "It may already be too late!"

Eve appeared, running along beside Sister Noel, face full of confusion.

"What's going on?" she said. "Is Father Ruiz okay?"

Zak handed her the scrap of paper with his orders. "We've got to get you out of here."

"I... I don't understand."

"Do you want to be O'Brien's wife?"

Her eyes widened. "No! He's a monster."

"Then come with us now."

He went to grab her hand, but she withdrew it.

"Where are we going? Who is this?" she said, noticing Barber who'd gone to the door to check outside.

"I am Master Sergeant Barber, Lady, and this is Mr. Wong, the head of the kitchen."

"You must go with the sergeant," Sister Greer said, taking her hands. "It is a matter of life and death."

"I... I... but..."

"Is there another way out?" Barber said. "They are coming this way. Many of them. Excisers."

Sister Noel said, "The sewers. I can guide you through them. My duties often involved such tasks." She shot a glance at the senior sister, then took Eve's hand. "Come. It will be unpleasant, but they will not follow us that way. Or, if they do, we will soon lose them."

"Hurry!" Barber called.

Wong stood alongside him. "I'll hold them off."

"No. If you do that, we will have no one inside the palace. Help me barricade this door, then go hide until they've passed. And you," he said, swinging to Zak, Eve and Sister Noel, "Go now! I'll follow."

Eve kissed Sister Greer who went to help build the barricade, then Zak took her hand, and they followed Sister Noel as she ran across the stone floor.

As they headed down the steps to the basement, they heard the sound of fists thumping on the door echoing through the orphanage.

Chapter 25

SEWER

"I'M NOT GOING DOWN there!" Eve yelled as Zak lifted the trap door leading to the sewers that ran beneath the orphanage.

"Fine," Sister Noel snapped. "Stay up here and become the concubine of that vile monster O'Brien. And you can watch as he sends each of us to the fire."

It seemed to Zak, young and naive as he was, that Eve was in some kind of a trance and simply denying the gravity of their plight. He let the trapdoor fall backward and held out his hand to her. "Please. Do it for us, and for Father Ruiz. He is going to fight O'Brien, but he can only do that if he knows you're safe." It *might* have been true, after all.

"I know it stinks," Sister Noel said, forcing herself to calm down and getting to the young girl's level. "I hated coming down here to begin with, but I survived. We must go."

From above and behind them came the sounds of thumping and scraping as if a press of people were pushing the barricade to one side.

"Come on!" Zak said, grabbing her hand and making his way down into the darkness.

It truly stank. If he hadn't been in mortal danger himself, he'd have baulked at coming down here even if meant humiliating himself in front of Eve. He felt his stomach contents rising in his throat as he heaved, but he somehow kept his mouth shut.

He reached the stone floor of the sewer and moved away from the bottom of the ladder to help Eve. They were in a long tunnel that was only just tall enough for him to stand in, and when Sister Noel stood beside him, she had to bend a little to keep her head clear of the top.

Darkness had fallen upon the stinking, slimy underworld as she'd pulled the trap door closed, and their only source of light was the flickering lantern in her hand.

"Come on," she said to Zak, indicating with her head that she expected him to take care of Eve. "We have to get through as quickly as we can. Someone's going to figure out where we've gone eventually. And be careful, it's slippery and you don't want to fall."

Eve let out a sob as he grabbed her hand, and he pushed down the anger he felt at the spoiled girl. It wasn't her fault. She was a victim who'd had a pampered childhood only to be sacrificed as she became a woman.

But when he tugged on her hand, she followed, and they made their slow, wet way through the sewers.

After what felt like hours but was probably no more than ten minutes, Zak spun around to look back the way they'd come. "I heard something."

"Oh my God, are there rats down here?" Eve shrieked.

Sister Noel snapped at her, "Quiet!" Then, speaking to Zak, she said, "Do you have a weapon?"

The dagger's silver blade glinted in the lantern light.

She nodded and they waited, until it was undeniable. Wet footsteps hurrying along behind them.

"We have to run!" Eve said.

Zak held up the knife. "Take her," he said to Sister Noel, feeling a surge of anger. "I'll deal with whatever's following us and catch you up."

For a moment it looked as though she would argue, but then she said, "Follow this tunnel until you reach an intersection. Take a right, then left again at the next. We'll wait as long as we can."

He felt her lips on his cheek and she was gone.

Zak pressed himself against the wall of the tunnel, finding he could squeeze himself behind a row of bricks that ran around the circumference. He gripped the handle of the knife, keeping it behind his body and out of sight.

Uneven steps approached. It was one person — almost certainly a man — and though Zak could see the light of a candle or lantern reflecting along the tunnel, his pursuer was walking slowly, as if unsure of his direction.

Farther along the tunnel, he could hear more sounds of pursuit. He should have run for it, but to do so now would give his position away and, after all, if he dealt with the first man, he might buy enough time to get through the sewers and out into the mercifully fresh air.

Splashes echoed, coming closer, but even so, he was surprised when the figure lurched out of the darkness. Instinctively, he threw himself at the man, who fell back under his attack, Zak landing on top of him in the half-filled channel of filth.

He raised the knife and swept it down as the lantern fell away, but a hand grasped his wrist.

"Stop!" a voice said. "You idiot. It's me!"

"Master Sergeant!" Zak almost fell over himself as he tried to get to his feet.

He helped the man up.

"We've got to go. Where are the others?"

"That way. I said I'd deal with you while they escaped."

"Good lad," Barber said. "Come on then."

Zak saw the blood coating his leather vest. "You're wounded!"

"We don't have time for this! Come on!"

He began limping along the tunnel, one arm pressed against his side and Zak overtook him, leading the way until they reached the first intersection.

The clamor behind grew louder as they struggled on, and by the time they found Sister Noel and Eve, it was obvious their pursuers were only minutes behind.

Noel was at the top of the ladder beneath an access hatch, obviously ready to open it if Zak had failed to keep the pursuers at bay. When she saw Barber, she immediately swung the trapdoor open, and Zak felt fresh air rush past him as he looked past her to the night sky beyond. A fine rain fell through the opening, but he had no time to enjoy it as Barber pushed him up the ladder.

He got on his belly and put his hand down to the master sergeant.

"Go," he said, looking up at Zak. "Get them out of here."

"No way!" Zak said. "I can't do it without you. Climb up!"

Barber smiled. "Yes you can. I can't make it."

Then Zak felt Eve settling on the wet cobbles beside him. "You promised Father Ruiz you'd take me somewhere safe. I thought you were a man of your word."

Barber's expression froze and Zak took the opportunity to push past Eve and jump down.

"What are you doing?" Barber said.

"Use my shoulders to climb up."

"They're coming, boy! Can't you hear them?"

"Then hurry."

Zak kept his voice calm, but the sounds of running that were growing louder and louder chilled his soul.

With a groan, Barber used his one good hand to begin heaving himself up, and Zak almost collapsed as the master sergeant's heavy boot pressed down on his shoulder.

Now he could hear shouting. They'd been seen!

With a yell, Barber's legs disappeared from view and Zak began climbing.

Shapes appeared, splashing along the tunnel, hands grabbing for Zak's feet. He felt himself being tugged down. He kicked down but the grip was as strong as iron.

The air around him exploded with a percussive bang and the tunnel emptied. He looked up, ears ringing, to see Master Sergeant Barber holstering his weapon and slamming the trapdoor shut as Zak launched himself onto the cobbles.

Barber pulled a tradesman's wagon over it, weighing it down.

"Idiot boy," he said, panting, hand clasped to his side.

Zak didn't care. He looked around, breathing heavily. They were beyond the perimeter of the university but far from safe. It was after curfew, so there was no one else on the streets, though surely the gunfire would bring trouble. They had a slim chance.

He turned to look at Eve and, in that moment, she squealed.

"Kurt!"

His former opponent, attempted assassin, and the young man Barber had persuaded him to pardon stood with a knife at her throat.

"Don't come no closer. Run if you like, I owe you that at least, but she's coming with me."

"Have you no honor?" Barber said, breathing heavily as he straightened up.

Kurt's eyes narrowed. "I have **nothing**. Better to have killed me than send me out onto the streets. But at least being a street-rat means I know the ways into the palace. I figured you'd come this way once the alarm was sounded."

"Let the girl go, Kurt. For your sake as much as hers. They won't reward you, you know."

"Maybe not, but I reckon I'll be taken to Father O'Brien to deliver his prize personally."

"Then what?"

"Then I'll fillet him for killing my father."

Barber shook his head. "You would condemn an innocent girl, so you get a chance at revenge?"

"Condemn? She'll live a life of luxury!"

"She'll live a life of pain and brutality."

Kurt began backing up, pulling Eve with him in the direction of the north gate. "Don't come any closer, I said!" Sister Noel had edged toward him, and Kurt swung Eve around and she squealed as his knife sliced the skin of her neck.

Zak surged forward, raising the sword above his head in a desperate attempt to get to her before Kurt cut her throat.

She dropped, blood defiling her neck and running down her white blouse.

Then she shrieked again.

But it was a shriek of rage. Something silver glinted in the light of the street lanterns and Kurt fell on his back, clutching at a black handle that stuck out of his chest.

His keening cry echoed from building to building and Zak saw people appearing in windows.

Noel pulled Eve away and shouted to Zak. "Deal with him. Now!"

Zak kneeled beside Kurt's writhing form and put his hand across the young man's mouth.

"Sorry," he said.

Kurt froze, looked him in the eye and, seeing death approaching began to say something. Then, as Zak's dagger stabbed into his chest beside Eve's stiletto, he went silent.

Shaking, Zak wiped his bloody hands on his pants, got to his feet and staggered over to where Master Sergeant Barber was leaning against a wall.

"Bring her!" he called over to Sister Noel.

Barber forced his eyes open, his face pallid. "Leave me."

"No way! You're coming with us."

And, as a steady rain diluted the blood staining the cobbles beneath Kurt, Zak guided them into the shadows.

Chapter 26

CONVOY

REUBEN LOOKED OUT FROM Lucifer's back over well-tended fields as they made their slow way north. The day after their near fatal encounter in Catlettsburg, they'd met a merchant caravan camped beside I-80. Howie had recognized one of the leaders and had managed to gain begrudging permission to join the convoy on condition that Reuben and Skeeter joined the scouts that scoured the land around the caravan for brigands as it crawled along.

There was no doubt they could have made faster progress without joining the convoy since it necessitated moving at the pace of the slowest member, but Reuben had seen enough evidence of the danger on these roads that he'd been content to sacrifice speed for safety.

He was on a small hill that overlooked a compact farming settlement protected by a high timber wall with lookout points on all four corners. People worked in the fields outside the walls, and a pair of oxen trudged back and forth dragging an iron plow, followed by their driver and a flock of small birds.

It looked a rich enough setting, but, even here, relatively close to the East Coast and north of the desert state of Texas, the farmers had to contend with a lack of water. Before the ecological catastrophe caused by the auroras, they'd have been able to rely upon rainfall to irrigate their crops, except for short periods in the occasional dry summer. Now, they'd been forced to dig a network of drainage channels to bring water from the sluggish rivers to the fields. The death of the Amazon rainforest had brought the planet to its knees.

For now, regions like this were able to produce enough food for their population, but vast areas of the North American continent, especially south of the thirty-fifth parallel, were deserts. Assuming humanity's population recovered — and that was a big assumption — food would be an increasing problem unless mankind could begin to rebuild its technology. And even with such a small population, there were times of extreme local hardship. The ecological damage done by the first two waves had led to massive surges in insect numbers that caused plagues of grasshoppers and other pests until nature temporarily restored the balance with an equally violent course correction. And the cycle continued, showing no signs of settling.

"You think they could hit us from here?"

Skeeter had brought his horse alongside Reuben and was pointing at the fortified farm.

The former exciser screwed up his eyes and put the battered pair of opera glasses to his better eye, looking through the one set of intact glass.

Something moved on the nearest lookout tower, and he saw that it was some kind of machine gun. M2, in all likelihood.

"Yeah, they could, but why waste the ammunition? We're no threat. Besides, I think they're for keeping the workers in line more than defense."

He'd seen this kind of operation many times over the years, most recently outside of Flowood. It was a form of indentured labor that would, forty years ago, have been simply known as slavery. The people working in the fields received food and protection and, in return, they gave their labor without expectation of pay, not even of the kind of scrip he'd seen used in Knoxville. As someone who'd been born into a free society before the fall, it made him feel sick to the stomach that people accepted this kind of a life and yet he understood why they did. If he'd known how things would turn out in advance, maybe he'd have valued his freedom a little more.

"We'd better catch up with the caravan," Reuben said, gesturing in the direction of the highway. "These people are no threat to us."

"Sure, boss," Skeeter said, leading the way.

Reuben gave one last look at the farm and put the fate of the peasants from his mind. It was a lovely spring day, and he could hear young birds chattering and squealing from the trees.

"AH, THERE YOU ARE, Jake."

Karl Sands, the caravan leader, smiled at Reuben as Bane pulled in alongside him at the head of the column. Skeeter had gone back to the middle of the convoy to check in with Asha and Howie. The little man was in his element, considering himself to be among his own people, though the other merchants seemed keen to maintain some distance.

"Karl."

"Anything to report?"

"There's a fortified farm a couple of miles to the east."

Karl nodded. "Sure. That's John McKnight's place. Him and his sons keep a tight hold over the poor devils who work in his fields."

"It wasn't pleasant to see."

"But we've got to keep our eyes on the job, am I right?"

Sands was in his early thirties, so he'd only known the world after the ruin, and he tended to look on people like Reuben with a mix of the derision often reserved for the old, and the fear of someone who has experienced what he never could. Sands would have heard tales of the former world all his life and yet the number of people who could relate those tales with firsthand knowledge was dwindling. Reuben didn't dare get his ebook reader out while they were with the convoy, or he and it would have been at immediate risk. Every man and woman in this convoy of traders would know its resale value.

"Nothing else on the road?"

"No. Has Carpenter completed his sweep?"

Bodie Carpenter was the lead shotgun for the caravan, along with two others, and therefore technically Reuben's senior, but Sands had enough sense to operate them separately as it was obvious that Carpenter resented Reuben's presence and, especially, his obvious competence.

"Still waitin' on him. You'll keep me company until he reports, won't you?"

Reuben sighed inwardly. It was past noon and he'd been in the saddle since just after dawn, scouting the lands to the east of the convoy. He wanted to eat and shut his eyes for a while, even if that meant the sort of half-sleep he'd become practiced in over the years he and Lucifer had been together. But he and the others were here by leave of Karl Sands, so he stayed.

"You was sayin' you came out of the West?"

"I did. Nevada."

Sands whistled. To him, any state on the other side of the Rockies was a source of amazement.

"But you must have traveled a lot in your line of work," Reuben said. He didn't want to talk about the West as it only reminded him of what he'd left there, and his mission.

"Sure, but you can cover a lot of miles if you just go around in a big circle. That's me. Man, I'd like to see more of the world. But you know what I'd like more?"

Reuben shrugged.

"A hot shower. I mean, one with real hot water, not just a bathtub with a hose. But I guess you remember, don't you?"

"Yes, I'm old enough."

Karl gazed into the distance. They were riding along the remains of I-80 which was in better condition here as there was enough traffic to keep the weeds at bay, though the asphalt had all but disappeared. Trees lined either side of the highway, with fields visible on the right and rough woodland on the left.

"I hear they have hot showers in New Boston. Kinda makes sense, I suppose, you get me?"

Reuben shrugged noncommittally. Karl was bouncing from one uncomfortable subject to another. He was correct, as it happened. The plumbing at Foundation headquarters was the very best around, as far as he knew, though few members of the order had private facilities.

"Wonder if we'll ever have hot showers again," Karl continued, getting minimal response. "Gotta happen someday, I figure. For now, though, all we can do is make sure the fellas behind us make it to Harrisonburg so they can bring a little..." he paused for a moment, picking his words, "sparkle to their lives, if you get my meaning."

"I don't, frankly."

Karl leaned across and shielded his mouth. "No disrespect, you understand? I mean, you're from the old world. Everyone did drugs back then, didn't they?"

"No. Are you saying that one of the merchants is carrying narcotics?"

Karl looked around sheepishly. "Nothin' heavy, just a little grass."

"How are you going to get it into the city?"

"Let's put it this way, there were seven carts when we set out, but there'll only be six when we get to the gate."

Reuben shook his head. Frankly, the less he knew about it the better. The last thing he wanted to do was attract attention to himself and his companions. He was just considering how to get himself out of the conversation so he could return to them when the shooting began.

Chapter 27

HOBBS

REUBEN SWUNG LUCIFER AROUND and headed toward the cracking of shots coming from the back of the convoy, Karl at his heels.

Skeeter joined them as they passed Howie and Asha who had turned on their mounts and were looking behind them.

"It's Carpenter!" Karl called.

Sure enough, Reuben could see the convoy's security officer on his horse with his two grunts beside him, all looking along the road.

"Boss," he said, turning at the sound of hooves.

"What's going on?" Karl said.

Carpenter's face was white, and sweat beaded along his forehead as he pointed back along the highway.

"Came out of nowhere," he said, shooting a poisoned glance at Reuben. "Hiding in the trees. Waited for us all to go past and jumped out at us. We chased them off, but they'll be back, I reckon."

Reuben nodded at the trees. "Who fired the first shot?"

He could see the answer written on Carpenter's face. He was a little older than Karl, but a whole lot meaner and with half the brains.

"This ain't our first ambush, Day," he spat. "And where were you, anyway?"

"Following orders. These riders didn't come from the east, did they? Because we scouted that way."

"This right, Bodie?" Karl said. "You shot first?"

Carpenter's face was tight with combined anger and frustration. "They jumped out at us, I told you!"

"They came from the west, like Jacob says, so how did they get the jump on us when you were supposed to be scouting that way?"

"Don't know where they came from, but they wasn't there when we checked!"

"Or maybe you didn't check careful enough. So help me God, Bodie Carpenter, if your itchy trigger finger has landed us in trouble, I'll shoot you myself."

Carpenter froze, seeing the threat in words that had been delivered almost jokingly. "We didn't kill none, Boss. We just winged a couple."

"Here they come," Karl said, speaking now to Reuben. "What do you think, Jake?"

Reuben squinted along the road where a pair of horsemen were sitting watching them. They clearly thought they were out of range, though Reuben would bet good money he'd be able to hit them with his 1911 and its original ammunition. "I think you'd better get your purveyor of medicinal delights to leave the caravan before they get here." Reuben said, "Maybe they're brigands, but they've got the smell of the law about them."

Karl nodded and barked orders to a man behind him.

Reuben turned to Skeeter. "Make sure Asha disappears without them noticing. Hide up in the woods, then come out once they've done."

"Sure, boss," the young man said, before turning his horse and riding along the column.

Cursing under his breath, Karl said, "I reckon you're right, Jake. Carpenter, you hang back. I'll deal with this."

If looks could kill, Reuben would have died on the spot as Carpenter relinquished his place.

Reuben said, "I suggest raising a white flag, unless you intend to fight."

"No way," Karl responded. "That'll only end badly." He looked at Carpenter who, after a moment's hesitation, turned and rode to the rear wagon and spoke to the merchant before returning with a light blue sheet.

"I guess it'll have to do," Karl said, holding it up high.

They all watched as the two riders kicked their mounts into a steady walk toward them, and Reuben could see many mounted figures behind them hanging back.

It was obvious which of them was the leader. It was the one with the trimmed yellow beard and finely polished silver badge. He looked like a reincarnated George Custer, with blond ringlets framing his neck beneath a wide brimmed hat. To complete the effect, he wore a buckskin coat and Reuben could see the ivory handle of a reversed revolver at his belt.

The rider beside him was dressed more modestly in brown canvas pants and hide jacket, and carried a modern replica repeater rifle.

"I am Lieutenant Hobbs of the Continental Rangers," the blond man said, in the voice and attitude of a man used to giving orders and having them instantly obeyed. "State your business here, and explain why you fired on my scouts."

He was looking directly at Reuben, who'd made the mistake of not walking Lucifer back behind Karl. "My name is Jacob Day, but Mr. Sands here leads this merchant caravan."

Karl thrust out his hand, but Hobbs ignored it.

"We're heading for Harrisburg, Lieutenant," Karl said. "You are welcome to inspect the convoy, of course, but we beg you to then allow us to carry on our way."

Karl's voice and manner had transformed. Reuben found himself re-evaluating his opinion of the young man. He had clearly dealt with men like Hobbs before.

"Shooting at our scouts is hardly the behavior of the innocent, Sands."

"I'm sorry," Karl said. "One of our men was startled. I hope there were no serious injuries and will be happy to compensate for the costs you've incurred. Can I offer you and your officers some refreshments?"

Hobbs laughed patronizingly. "Officers? Oh, Bowden here is merely my batman."

Reuben saw the man's eyes narrow at his master's dismissiveness.

"Bowden, ride back and tell Sergeant Gallo to make a temporary camp. He is then to bring a squad under his command to inspect the convoy. Inform our guest, also."

Bowden saluted, turned his horse and rode away.

For a split second, Karl glanced at Reuben and saw resignation there and he understood that a ritual was taking place, a ritual that would leave Karl poorer but, hopefully, able to continue.

Reuben forced himself not to look toward the woods where, all being well, Skeeter hid with Asha, merely exchanging a nod with Howie who looked at the visitor on his dun horse with suspicion and fear.

As they made it back to the front of the convoy, Karl yelled for his fixer, a man called Short who climbed down from the first wagon, followed moments later by his wife, a pair Reuben had never seen apart for more than a moment. Short was a grubby, subservient man who was old enough to have seen the apocalypse, and his wife was smaller, younger and meaner.

She took the reins of the horses, tied them to the wagon, and disappeared inside, returning moments later with three cups of black ladled from a large pot she kept in the back of the wagon.

Karl helped the lieutenant climb down from his horse, and they stood looking along the caravan as they waited for the male Short to rig the large tent used as a communal mess when the convoy camped.

From beyond the last wagon, they could see figures marching. "That's Gallo. A good man. Efficient, but unimaginative. Not suited for command at all. But then, there can only be one chief? You know this, Mr.? I'm sorry, I've forgotten your name."

Reuben saw Karl color as he fought to keep his temper. "Sands. Karl Sands."

"Excellent black," the lieutenant said, apparently oblivious to Karl's mood. "Almost as good as coffee. And what is your function?" he said, turning to Reuben.

"I'm heading for Harrisonburg and, since the caravan is going the same way, I joined."

"These are, indeed, dangerous times," Hobbs said. "Brigands roam these lands and, though we hunt them when we can, there are too few of us."

"Is that your mission?" Reuben asked, watching soldiers disappearing into the first wagon. "To hunt bandits?"

Hobbs shook his head, causing his curly yellow hair to oscillate, generating an aroma of cinnamon. "No, we have been on Federal business, establishing the disposition of the towns and cities in this region. We were on our way back to DC when we picked up our passenger, also seeking the protection of numbers."

They watched as the soldiers left the rearmost wagon and moved onto the next one. Reuben hadn't spoken to all the merchants, but Karl was wise enough to have the least valuable wagon — and the one that had paid the least to be part of the convoy — at the rear. He'd spoken briefly to the wagon's owner; a man in his late middle years who was returning from the south with a small consignment of dried fruit that looked hardly worth the effort to transport to Harrisonburg.

The second one had textiles, and Reuben imagined the illicit goods were contained in the third or fourth wagons and had been spirited into the woods while they'd been talking with the lieutenant. At least, he hoped they had been.

Howie and his mule were next, and Reuben ground his teeth, hoping that the little man didn't have anything illegal with him or, if he had, he'd hidden it effectively.

He breathed again as the soldiers moved to the next wagon. He seemed to remember that it had a shipment of powders for dying clothes. Perhaps that was where the illicit substances had been hidden.

They were finishing their black, and Lieutenant Hobbs was enjoying a dried apple from Karl's personal store, when they saw a man with sergeant's stripes approach Hobbs and salute.

"Yes, Sergeant Gallo? Did you find anything?"

"Nothing illegal, sir," he said.

Hobbs nodded. "Thank you. Return and form up the men."

"Yes, sir. They'll pay the toll, will they, sir?"

Irritation flashed in Hobbs' eyes.

"Don't be so impertinent, Gallo! Carry out my orders and form up the men."

After a moment's hesitation, the sergeant spun on his heels and marched away.

Reuben examined the face of the lieutenant as he turned back to Karl. He saw anger there. And he saw fear. This man's authority was fragile. If Reuben could bring himself to believe it, he'd imagine that the lieutenant commanded only with the consent of his men.

"I will have the man flogged," he said. "But he is not incorrect. We are required to exact a toll for permitting caravans such as this one to use the state highway network."

"Are you kidding me?" Reuben said, unable to hold his incredulity at bay.

He felt Karl's hand on his arm. "It's okay. It's standard practice. We'll be happy to pay a reasonable tariff. Would one hundred bits be sufficient?"

The lieutenant rubbed his bearded chin as he considered this. No doubt he was working out how far a hundred bits would go between his men. He shook his head. "Five bits each?"

So, there were a maximum of twenty, though Reuben doubted the lieutenant intended to split it equally if he could possibly avoid it.

"Two hundred would be more satisfactory."

"Two hundred is too much," Karl said, obviously fighting to keep his temper from spilling over. "I will offer no more than one fifty."

"We could take it all," Hobbs said.

Reuben shook his head. "Not without much loss."

"Who's that?" Karl said, his attention seized by movement at the back of the column.

Hobbs spun around, then cursed under his breath. "That is Macias."

"Who's he?"

Reuben's heart froze.

"He is an exciser."

Chapter 28

MACIAS

REUBEN FOLLOWED AS KARL accelerated on his horse, with Hobbs in close pursuit. Of all the rotten luck. His first thought was for Asha, and he prayed that Skeeter had gotten him away. His second thought was for himself. Was this one of those sent to hunt him?

He brought Lucifer to a halt behind the others, trying to shield his black gelding from view.

The exciser was a much younger man and fresh out of the seminary, Reuben judged. He sat as he'd been trained, perfectly still, and waited with staged patience until his audience was fully assembled. Sergeant Gallo stood beside his stirrup, his attention mainly on Hobbs, as if he wanted some indication of whether the negotiation had gone well, but the lieutenant blanked him, focusing his attention only on the exciser.

"My name is Macias," the young man said, looking at Karl. "I represent the Foundation. It has been alleged that your caravan contains within it an enemy of God. One whose very form mocks the creator. An agent of the devil."

Karl shook his head, but Reuben could see and hear the fear. "There's no one like that. And who's done the accusing?"

Macias gestured beyond the line of wagons until a figure emerged reluctantly from their shadow.

"Carpenter, what the hell?" Karl spat.

A spasm of shock and anger at the curse passed over Macias' face, but he mastered himself as Carpenter nudged his horse toward them.

"Mr. Sands don't know nothin' about it," Carpenter said, before looking at Karl. "I'm sorry, I should've told you before now, but he begged me not to say nothin'."

"Who?"

"Perhaps you'd better show us, Carpenter," Macias said.

Reuben was paralyzed with fear. Had Howie given him or Asha away somehow?

Carpenter nudged his horse backward expertly, then, as he passed the rearmost wagon, his arm shot out and a gray-haired figure fell to the ground with a cry.

"It is him?" Macias said, hunger and excitement written into his face.

"Please! Leave me alone!" the old man said, his terror obvious.

Carpenter shook his head. "No sir, it's what he's got hid in the back of his wagon. That's what you gotta see."

Climbing down from his horse, Macias moved swiftly to the steps of the canvas-colored wagon and gestured to Sergeant Gallo, who climbed inside.

After a few minutes of stomping around, he called out, "Nothing here, sir."

Reuben's fear had been replaced by puzzlement. What was going on?

"There's a space under the driver's seat," Carpenter said.

"It's too small!" Gallo called. "Oh, my G—"

Macias swooped inside as Reuben heard the sound of splintering wood.

There was a shriek of fear, followed by Macias's voice yelling in sudden horror before he got himself under control.

The old man had run around to the entrance. "Don't hurt him, please!" he cried out. "He's just a boy."

"No," Macias said, as he emerged from the wagon. "He is a monster."

And, into the daylight stepped a face out of nightmares. To begin, Reuben thought he must be a victim of a dreadful fire, but then he realized that the child showed no signs of pain, he was merely terrified. What had seemed to be burns were, in fact, something like scales with lines of livid red between them as if, at any moment, his face might burst open.

The child was revolting, and, for a moment, Reuben's only thought was that the creature should be put to the fire for everyone's sake.

And then he took a breath, saw the terror, and the person behind those all-too-human eyes.

This was a child, and it was all he could do to stop himself tearing the boy from Gallo's repulsed grasp. There was no hope that way. If he was to act, given that the exciser had a company of men at his call, it would have to be when there was at least a chance of success.

So, he sat and watched, hands gripping tight on Lucifer's reins as the monster-child was dragged away.

"YOU ARE RESPONSIBLE FOR this!" Macias said to Karl, jabbing a finger at him.

Lieutenant Hobbs' men had taken over the convoy and were, even now, using the mutant's discovery as a pretext to loot every wagon.

Karl had been disarmed, and was sitting with his hands on his head, beside the campfire. He wasn't bound, but his eye had swollen when Sergeant Gallo had punched him at Macias' instruction.

Reuben had given up his cap and ball revolver, but had hidden his 1911 in his saddle bag, and the soldiers hadn't yet rifled through that. Not that he'd be able to do much with it.

"I didn't know," Karl said.

Reuben admired the man. Karl had a stoic courage it had been hard to imagine when they'd been chatting together before the soldiers first appeared.

But as for Carpenter. If Reuben survived this, that traitor wouldn't. He'd clearly betrayed them hoping for a monetary reward, and he'd almost certainly succeeded in that. But Reuben Bane would make him choke on the thirty pieces of silver he'd taken to sell out his employer and the poor child who was now shackled and gagged and guarded by men without mercy.

Reuben remained in the shadows, largely disregarded by the soldiers wandering back and forth while the merchants sat together in a disconsolate huddle.

He felt a tug on his arm and turned to see Howie looking up at him. "No sign of them," he whispered.

Reuben grunted an acknowledgment. That, at least, was good news. "You had no trouble?"

Howie gave a tiny shrug. "No more than usual. Paid them off."

"I don't want to know any more."

Their attention was drawn by the old man who'd sheltered the boy being dragged to stand in front of the exciser. His face was bruised, and blood ran down from his cheek bone to stain his white beard.

"What is your name?"

"What ... what are you gonna do with the boy?"

The exciser's hand flew and caught the old man's face. Then he calmly took a scrap of white cloth from his pocket and wiped the blood from his fingers. "I ask the questions," he said, his voice unnaturally calm. Reuben recognized a professional psychopath when he saw one.

"Your name," he repeated. "Withholding it achieves nothing but further pain."

The old man slumped a little. "Gene. Gene Burrell."

"And the beast? What is its name?"

"He's not an animal, he's a boy."

Macias' face twisted in rage. "It is an abomination! An insult to God's perfect creation! It will burn!"

"No, please."

"It will burn and those who aided it will join it in the flames. Do you not fear such a painful end?"

Burrell nodded.

"Then answer my questions and your death will be quick and merciful."

The old man sobbed.

"What is its name?" Macias repeated.

"R... Roberto. He's called Roberto. But he can't help how he is."

"It's not the cockroach's fault it is what it is. And yet we tread it under foot without thought. Now, how did you come to have this thing in your care?"

Shaking his head, Burrell said in a voice so low that Ruben could barely make out his words. "I... I found him wandering, north of here. I was heading West..."

"To the ungoverned lands, of course."

"Yes, master. He was going to come with me, but he got sick. Said the only person who could help him was his mother."

"He has a mother? She is like him?"

Burrell shook his head again. "No."

"How could she help him? Speak!" The hand lashed out and, again, Macias fastidiously wiped it clean as the prisoner moaned.

Macias whispered to Gallo who disappeared then, moments later, returned with the boy. He was dressed in crude sack cloth and his head was covered with a canvas bag, but there was no mistaking him as he sobbed and yelled in obvious terror.

Gallo held him tight beside the campfire.

"Speak now or he goes to the fire this very night!"

Burrell made for a wretched sight as he shook his head, unable to back away because he was held tight by a guard.

The boy shrieked as Gallo edged him to the margins of the fire.

"SPEAK!"

"She... she's a scientist. She's curing him."

Reuben's insides froze solid.

For a moment, even Macias seemed lost for speech, then he yelled one word at the top of his voice, silencing everyone as it faded away.

"Witch!"

Chapter 29

ROBERTO

AS THE SUN ROSE behind the trees on the eastern side of the highway, Reuben threw off his traveling blanket and checked on Lucifer. The horse snorted, nuzzling Bane's hand as he ran it up the animal's face before hooking the nose bag into place.

"That's the last of it, old fella," he said, looking along the wagon train to where soldiers were milling lazily around in the morning light.

Soldiers? In contrast to the fastidious Lieutenant Hobbs, his men were little more than a rabble. They could almost be a band of brigands using Hobbs to lend them a veneer of legitimacy and authority. But there were two score of them, and many looked like battle-hardened scrappers.

And Carpenter had joined them, no longer even pretending to be working for Karl Sands.

As for the caravan leader, he cut a forlorn figure and had been confined to the wagon he shared with Mr. and Mrs. Short. He knew he no longer had any control over what happened next, he had to simply wait and see what was left of his caravan by the time the soldiers left.

But Reuben's mind and sympathy were reserved exclusively for the mutant boy and the man who'd been protecting him.

Gene Burrell had been beaten unconscious during the interrogation without revealing anything more about the identity of the female scientist linked with the mutant boy. Macias, it seemed, was an inexperienced torturer and had allowed his anger to get the better of him.

But Reuben was in no doubt. The monster's mother was Hannah Myers, the woman he'd been sent east to find. The woman that her former husband, the mayor of New Haven, said was crucial to the future of that outpost of civilization and, perhaps much more.

So, Reuben had resolved to make sure Burrell didn't reveal her name or location to the exciser and that meant he would probably have to kill the old man.

Bane had made his camp as close to the tent that Macias and the guards had taken over as he could, and he was confident that the old man hadn't been interrogated again yet, but movement within the tent had woken him.

A bugle sounded, waking the rest of the camp, and Reuben did his best to disappear into the gap between two wagons while keeping a good view as, after a few minutes, Gene Burrell stumbled into the daylight, supported on both sides by guards.

He looked half dead, and Reuben ran his fingers along the cold, reassuring metal of the 1911. What was he going to do? All he knew for sure was that he couldn't allow Burrell to reveal Hannah's location, but what about the mutant boy?

He wished he could convince himself that Roberto was in enough pain from his mutation that death would be a mercy, but he couldn't. He'd only seen him briefly, but, other than his disfigured face, he saw nothing wrong with the boy. It was tough to override his bestial loathing for such a hideous appearance. But it was tougher to ignore his pity. It was as with Asha, but dialed up to eleven — Asha could be disguised and kept from the attention of any but the most thorough examiner. One look at Roberto's face and it was obvious that he was a mutant.

A few years ago, that would have been the end of it for Reuben. This boy was a mutant and his genes had to be eliminated from the gene pool for the sake of humanity. But then Reuben's daughter had been born with an extra digit, and the house of cards had instantly collapsed. He felt ashamed that it had taken a personal experience to change his view to one that, now, seemed obvious.

Roberto was a deviant. He was a mutant, but he was also a human being. He was just a boy and, as he was dragged squealing and sobbing toward a clear area of grass beside the road where the soldiers were gathering dry wood into a pile, it was all Reuben could do to stop himself intervening.

But what would that achieve? There were too many. Even with the element of surprise, even with Howie's help, he'd be overwhelmed in a matter of seconds and the boy would burn anyway.

He ground his teeth, wincing as he dug his fingernails into the flesh of his palm and watched as Macias emerged, following the solemn procession.

Reuben caught sight of the flamboyant Lieutenant Hobbs who looked as though he'd rather be anywhere else as two stakes were dragged out of the trees. They were young silver birch that had been crudely stripped of their branches. The end of each was shaped into a rough point and the stakes were lowered into holes dug in the soft earth, and the two victims were tied to them. Roberto's hood was left in place, but Burrell's bruised and bloodied face was clear for all to see.

Kindling was piled against both, and Reuben, feeling he had to at the very least bear witness moved closer, finding himself standing beside Karl. The caravan wrangler turned to look at Reuben out of lifeless eyes. He shook his head, and Reuben understood immediately. He couldn't process what had happened since the day before when he'd been a confident young man running a lucrative, but essential, business and, perhaps, even contemplating a bright, wealthy future. He'd thought he could deal with the soldiers, but the presence of the exciser had changed everything.

"We give praise and thanks to God for revealing these defilers, causing them to crawl from their hiding places to be exposed to the bright light of righteousness," Macias began, almost chanting the words as the gathered audience of soldiers and wagon drivers went silent.

"And you are blessed and honored in the sight of our Lord as you witness the purification ceremony. But be warned," he said, his voice rising as he basked in the attention of his audience and pointed at the pathetic figure of Gene Burrell, "of the consequences of sheltering such abominations."

With that, Reuben sensed movement from behind and Karl Sands was thrust to the ground, then grabbed by two guards and hauled to his feet.

"This man will also face punishment. He will share their fate."

A rumbling went up from the crowd of waggoners and, for a moment, Macias hesitated, but at a word from Lieutenant Hobbs, the soldiers standing beside him snapped their rifles to their eyes and silence fell again.

Reuben found himself looking down the barrel of a rifle that was pointing directly at him. It shook gently, and he looked beyond it to see the nervous face of the man holding the weapon.

Macias was the only person present who obviously wanted to be here, and they were all held there by the force of his will.

Gently, Howie maneuvered his small frame into the space Karl Sands had occupied, and Reuben noticed that the Shorts stood behind him, each with stony, unreadable faces. Perhaps they thought their erstwhile master was about to get his comeuppance.

Sands had been brought to stand alongside the shaking figure of Roberto. No stake was brought for him, but Hobbs had moved beside him, his revolver drawn, ready, it seemed to do the exciser's bidding.

They were all toys of Macias, puppets to his sadistic whim.

"You have one final opportunity," he said to Burrell. "Tell me where I will find this witch, and I will reward you by making your death swift, and the monster's. Refuse, and you will both die in torment."

At that moment, he nodded to one of the soldiers who raised a cloth covered stick and put a match to it. Immediately, it burst into flame, and the soldier lowered it into the bundle of twigs at Burrell's feet. Then he ripped the hood from Roberto's head and the watchers gasped as the full horror of his mutation was revealed.

"You see?" Macias screeched. "You see? He is a monster!"

Then, as the fire caught and began to crackle, he returned to Burrell and said, "This is your last chance. Tell me where she lives or the boy burns in front of your eyes.

Burrell shook his head and sobbed, as Roberto screamed in terror.

And Reuben acted.

He raised his Colt to the heavens and fired a single shot.

"No, he will not burn!"

As the echo died away, the only sound was the crackling of the flames.

"My name is Exciser Reuben Bane and you, Macias, are a heretic!" he yelled, striding toward where Macias stood, rooted to the spot.

Like a striking snake, Reuben thrust his arm around the exciser's throat and pressed the revolver to his temple. "Stand back or I shoot!"

Chapter 30

SNAKE

REUBEN BACKED AWAY, DRAGGING Macias with him. The exciser was snarling with rage, but stopped struggling as Reuben pressed the Colt into the skin of his temple.

Now what was he going to do?

The truth was, he had no idea. But sometimes the act of resistance is more important than the result. At least Gene Burrell and Roberto would know, as they died, that someone had risked everything to help them.

Gallo had leveled his rifle, and, on Reuben's other side, Lieutenant Hobbs was aiming his white handled revolver directly at a point between Bane's eyes.

"Release him, you fool," Hobbs said. He had the air of a man who doesn't understand what just happened and was acting entirely on impulse.

"You will burn!" Macias snarled, trying to twist around to face Reuben who had him in a tight headlock. "You are a traitor to the Foundation."

"And you're a traitor to mankind."

Then Reuben felt the cold steel of a rifle barrel pressing into his ribs, and Gallo's voice said, "Do as the lieutenant says, or I'll blow your lungs out your ribcage."

Reuben held his breath, cursing his impetuosity, but gripping the exciser tight. He waited for sudden pain and the end of things.

Then a shot rang out and Gallo fell.

Reuben looked to the wagons where Howie disappeared, overwhelmed by soldiers, his rifle discarded. The Shorts surged forward. Mr. Short held a snub-nosed revolver and he fired into the press of soldiers surging toward Reuben and Macias.

As he tried to keep the exciser between himself and the approaching enemy, Reuben saw Mrs. Short raising a shotgun and firing into the remaining soldiers, felling several in a hail of buckshot.

Then Karl was at his shoulder, released by Mr. Short who handed him a spare weapon.

Through all this, Lieutenant Hobbs stood, his revolver pointing first at Reuben, then at Short, then moving from target to target, but shooting no one.

Around Reuben, the air filled with black smoke and the percussive bangs of concentrated fire as he retreated, still using the snarling Macias as a shield.

"Help them, quick!" he said, risking a glance at the two figures staked to the spikes, flames rising around them.

Then Skeeter emerged from the woods beyond where the two figures stood. "Got it, boss," he shouted.

"Follow me," Karl said, pulling on Reuben's arm. They headed for the highway, walking backwards, keeping the advancing soldiers covered as they went.

Beside the highway, provisions had been unpacked by the Shorts in barrels. Karl ducked down in the cover provided and took aim at the soldiers now moving along the wagon-train, led by Lieutenant Hobbs, whose face was a livid red.

Reuben threw Macias to the ground, then helped Gene Burrell guide the mutant Roberto into the transient shelter provided. Despite his scarred face, Reuben could see he was in shock, but Bane's focus was entirely on the soldiers who had found their own cover.

In the margins of the woods, Reuben glimpsed the wagon-drivers hiding, waiting to see which way the battle would go.

Reuben turned to Skeeter, who was now crouching beside him. "What are you doing here? Where's Asha?"

"He told me to come," Skeeter said. "He's hiding safe enough. Hey, where's Howie?"

"I don't know. He shot Gallo, but I lost sight of him."

"Hope he makes it."

"I hope we all make it."

"Ha!" Macias said. "None of you will escape the flame!"

Reuben ignored the exciser. He was probably right. They were outnumbered many times over, and there was nothing to stop Hobbs splitting his forces and using one group to keep them pinned down, and the other to outflank them.

Then the lieutenant stepped boldly out from the cover of the wagons. "Who leads you?" he called, having recovered his composure.

Reuben looked at Karl, and Karl looked back.

Bane stood, while Sands kept Macias under control.

"My name is Reuben Bane."

"That is not the name you gave when we met."

"It has been necessary to travel under another identity. Reuben Bane is my true name." A lie. Thirty-five years ago, he'd been called Justin. But that boy was long dead.

"You declared yourself an exciser."

"A lie!" Macias called out. "He is a renegade! Even now he is hunted by the blessed Foundation." Macias went silent as Karl put a knife to his throat.

Hobbs waved at the men behind him. "It is not my place to interfere in Foundation matters, so you will surrender and submit to investigation and justice."

"No, we will not."

"You are outnumbered. Our victory is inevitable."

"Then be my guest," Reuben said before ducking under cover again, and crouching beside Karl.

"Take him away," Karl said to Mr. Short, gesturing at the exciser. "If he tries anything, blow his brains out."

Short nodded and dragged the protesting Macias into the doubtful cover of a bush.

"He's right, they do outnumber us," Karl said.

Reuben nodded. "If he was a competent commander, then I'd agree our situation is pretty hopeless, but he's neither competent nor in command."

"What do you mean?"

"You might not have noticed, but his revolver isn't even loaded."

Reuben watched the retreating lieutenant as Karl simply stared at him.

"If his men don't trust him enough to give him a loaded weapon, what's the chance that they'll follow his orders?"

And, as if they'd heard him speak, he saw the troops nearest them turn and walk away, gathering their loot as they went.

"Those sons of bitches," Karl spat.

Reuben put his hand on Sands' shoulder, keeping him from breaking cover. "Leave it. They do out-number us, and even if they won't rescue Macias, they'll certainly defend their plunder if we try to take it from them."

Karl relaxed and nodded.

Then a scream rent the air.

"Short!"

"Macias!" Reuben said, getting to his feet and run-ning for the bushes Short had hidden the exciser in.

The fixer lay on his back writhing and moaning with a knife handle sticking out of his chest, blood staining his shirt.

"Jumped me," he gasped as his wife kneeled beside him, filling the air with curses as she examined the wound.

"Which way did he go?" Karl asked.

But Reuben was already moving, heading deeper into the trees, searching for any signs of the exciser, and cursing. Just as it had seemed they'd survived, the cause of the danger had wriggled free like a rattlesnake. He couldn't be allowed to escape, or he'd dog their every step.

There was no sign.

Stop. No point in blundering through the wood. Think. Where would he go?

Of course. He'd look for the protection of the sol-diers. Reuben glanced back toward the highway to orient himself, then ran parallel to it, immediately rewarded by seeing the obvious trampling of a man seeking the quickest way back to safety.

Reuben accelerated, eyes searching ahead for any sign of the exciser.

Then something took his legs out from under him, and he fell face first in the leaf mold and dirt.

As he began to roll, a heavy weight landed on his back.

"Die!"

Reuben twisted and saw the flash of a knife pass by his cheek. He kicked upwards and was rewarded by a howl of pain as Macias fell away.

But the young exciser was as fast as a striking serpent. He caught himself, turning his momentum into a swinging, scything thrust of the knife as Reuben threw himself backwards, watching the blade fly past.

There was no time to draw and fire his pistol and, in any case, a gunshot might bring the soldiers running. He'd left his sword strapped to Lucifer's saddle, and a sudden fear gripped him, even in the midst of a battle for his life, that the soldiers might have taken the horse as part of their loot.

Macias thrust, his movements a blur. He was a truly accomplished knifeman, well trained at the Foundation academy, but Reuben was a veteran of a hundred battles, and he kicked out at the young exciser's arm, knocking the blade from his hands and launching at him.

Somehow, Macias was ready, grabbing Reuben's collar and vaulting the older man into the trunk of a tree to one side, the knife knocked from his hands and flying away.

Macias was on top of him, fingers wrapped around Reuben's throat.

He cried out in pain as the exciser squeezed his Adam's apple, then a large stone appeared in Macias' other hand and he brought it down with savage force, but Reuben had managed to move his head so that it only struck a glancing blow, ripping the skin on the side of his head and stunning him.

Instinct took over and he flung his arm across, catching his opponent on the temple. Reuben roared as he threw himself at Macias, his momentum driving the man back. He swung his fist and caught the exciser on the cheek, then rained blows down on him as their fight descended into a bestial brawl.

Finally, he had the snarling, raging younger man under control.

"You... you are a heretic," Macias said, panting. "Kill me, or I will hunt you... to the ends... of the Earth. You and... those you love."

Reuben picked up the same jagged stone that Macias had tried to break his skull with.

"And you are an evil fool, who will bring nothing but suffering to the world. Macias, I sentence you to death."

The young exciser's eyes widened as he saw it coming and, as Reuben brought the stone down, the exciser raised his hands and the stone caught him on the side of the head, knocking him unconscious, though much of its power had been deflected.

Reuben searched around on the ground for the heavy stone. It would be a just execution — unlike what Macias had wanted to inflict on Roberto — and the world would be a better place without him in it. But the same could have been said of a twenty-five-year-old Reuben Bane, and he'd been spared to become a better man.

He couldn't do it.

And then a shadow appeared at his shoulder.

Asha handed him the stone.

"He is a bad man. He has no good in him. If you don't kill him, he will hunt us until we are dead."

Reuben looked into the boy's eyes, seeking the source of Asha's certainty. It was as if he saw an old soul looking out at him.

Macias had to die.

Reuben lifted the stone again and, as he brought it down, he prayed for forgiveness.

"No!"

The stone plunged into the dirt, and he looked up to see Lieutenant Hobbs staring down at him in wonder, a soldier holding a weapon at his side.

"He is evil," Reuben said, feeling bitterness rising within him.

"I don't doubt that, but he's also valuable. The Foundation will pay well for his return, assuming he survives."

Reuben looked down at the young man. Blood poured from the wound at this temple, and he was certain he'd felt the cracking of bone. It was the kind of wound that is more dangerous than it looks at first. Nine times out of ten, it would result in death. Even if he woke up, Macias faced a long healing process and the ever-present risk of blood poisoning.

"He has value even if he doesn't survive," Reuben said. "The Foundation will thank you for returning his body.

"Ah, but they won't pay as handsomely. Now, please leave him and we will take it from here."

Reuben looked up at Hobbs as he got off the unconscious exciser. "What kind of a man are you? You're no better than a leader of brigands."

Hobbs smiled and shrugged. "I am the kind of man who isn't going to put a bullet in your brain for impertinence. I'd take that and go if I were you."

And so, Reuben stood by as Macias was lifted by a couple of soldiers and taken away.

He hoped with every fiber of his being that he never saw him again.

Chapter 31

LOIS

HANNAH SAT ON THE front seat of the cart, heading to the makeshift infirmary that was set up in the former elementary school just outside the center of the city.

She'd handed the reins to Jenson Spillane, the young boy who'd been sent to fetch her. Born into this new agrarian world, driving a horse and cart was second nature to him whereas Hannah had grown up at a time when cars were learning to drive themselves and needed little attention and even less skill to operate.

Her heart was thumping in her chest as she wished the couple of miles journey was over. Lois Neff had woken up, the boy had said.

Jumping down from the cart, she jogged inside, heading past the masked amateur nurses who didn't stop her because she was a familiar visitor now. She'd pulled her FFP2 mask out of her pocket and slowed down. It wouldn't do to hyperventilate. This could be her moment.

The door of the vice-principal's office was open, and Hannah could see Ida Beale lurking in the entrance. Ida looked around as she approached, but

Hannah didn't acknowledge her. It wasn't her old friend she was here to see.

She breathed out a huge gasp of relief as she saw that Lois was sitting up, but was stopped in her tracks when the patient looked up at her.

"You bitch!" she yelled, before collapsing in a coughing fit.

"Now then," Ida said. "She only did what she thought was best."

Hannah's jaw dropped. Sure, she'd expected a little pushback from the diminutive doctor, but this level of invective had taken her entirely by surprise.

It was only then that she saw who was sitting next to the doctor.

"Sheriff Mendez, please arrest this woman on charges of violating my bodily autonomy," Lois said.

The face of Raul Mendez made it obvious that he would rather have been anywhere but in this room, right now. "But she saved your life."

"That isn't the point! She injected me without my permission."

Hannah finally snapped out of her catatonic state. "Are you serious? Dead people don't have any rights. You're only alive because of me!"

"There's a principle at stake, Doctor Myers. Some principles are more important than life or death."

Jabbing a finger at her, Hannah spat, "And one of those principles is serving your community. You're the only person who can help me do that, so make any complaint you like, once the emergency is over. But, for now, get better, get out of that bed and get making penicillin."

"IT'S GOING TO BE bloody difficult for us to work together if you won't talk to me." Hannah sat beside
the bed as Lois Neff studiously ignored her.

Neff's mood hadn't been improved by Sheriff
Mendez's lack of interest in arresting Hannah. Her
histrionics had finally pushed him past his limit, and
he'd gone off to try to maintain order with a rapidly
diminishing police force.

The doctor was, at least, obviously improving. The
buboes on her neck had shrunk and, though they
didn't look remotely normal, at least they weren't
threatening to burst at any moment.

"You aren't the first person to violate me," Lois
said, still avoiding eye contact.

Hannah exhaled. "I'm sorry to hear that, Lois, I
really am. But you must have treated patients when
they weren't able to give their consent, if it was life
and death."

"Sure, I've used a cold compress to relieve fever
in an unconscious patient. I've even bullied a sick
person to take their meds when they didn't want to.
But I've never stuck a needle into anyone without
their knowledge. Breaking the skin, that's the line I
never cross."

Then, finally, she looked in Hannah's direction,
her eyes moist. "You think I'm irrational. That's fair
enough."

"I can only say I'm sorry so many times," Hannah
said. "But I'm glad you're recovering, and if it's at
the cost of our friendship, then that's a price I'm
prepared to pay."

"Friendship requires trust, and you lost that when
you put a needle in my arm."

The chair creaked under Hannah as she got to her
feet. "Our city needs us so, friends or not, we need

to work together. Can you put your anger with me to one side for long enough for that?"

She headed for the door and turned, holding Lois's gaze as the doctor gave a tiny nod.

"HOW MANY SHARPS DO we have?"

Hannah looked up from the kitchen table as Lois came in, speaking without preamble. It had been three days since she'd gotten out of bed, and Hannah had used the time to step up production of her anti-viral treatment. Ida had put out a call for any and all surviving glassware that could be used for culturing. It had proven more difficult than Hannah had hoped, but easier than she'd feared, the main problem being that the granulocytes needed very precise temperature control to grow effectively and the larger the culture vessel, the harder that was to achieve.

So, rather than wrestle with that problem, she'd opted to grow each batch separately. It did, at least, make keeping count simple since each represented one dose. She'd taken inventory that morning, and they had enough to treat a dozen people, though that was barely a tenth of those who were sick.

"If you mean hypodermic syringes," she said, not looking up, "I've got two boxes of a hundred left."

Lois put a large bottle of a milky fluid on the table. "Good, though we'll have to use them multiple times each."

Hannah winced at the thought. Lois was right enough — the boxes of syringes were from before the fall, and she hadn't heard of anyone who was making replacements. A problem for another day. "At least the antibiotics will be easy enough. We've got enough spoons, after all." The smile bounced off the doctor's fixed expression.

"There's no time to dry it, so that means there's not as much here as it might seem. Probably enough to treat fifty people."

Hannah nodded. "It's a start. Has Mitch had any yet?"

"Yes, he was compos mentis when I saw him last. Just about. He's not getting any worse, and sometimes he's completely lucid."

"Is Ida with him?"

"No, Councilor Espinoza is sitting with him. He's been at Councilor Snider's side for days."

Hannah looked up at her. "He has? Atoning for his sins, perhaps?"

Lois made no response, but neither did she make any move to leave.

Finally, Hannah had had enough. "What's on your mind, Doctor?"

"We talked about trust."

"Did we? Well, you told me I'd betrayed your trust. I don't remember making much of a contribution."

Neff tightened, but didn't bite back. "Tell me who Roberto is."

"What?"

"The name on the vial you injected yourself with. You didn't tell me when I asked, and then I got sick myself."

"Does it matter?"

Neff's eyes narrowed. "I don't know, does it? Seems to me that if it's unimportant, you wouldn't be afraid to tell me."

Hannah put down her pipette and focused her attention on her former friend.

Before she could reply, Neff said, "You can trust me. Whatever you're hiding, whoever you're protecting. I won't tell anyone."

"Roberto is my son."

Neff looked around as if expecting him to appear out of the shadows.

"He's not here. He ran away when the Foundation came to town."

"Why? I mean, sure, many of us felt like skipping town."

Hannah examined Neff's expression. Was this a test? Would their friendship thaw again if she showed she was prepared to trust? Was that sufficient reason to reveal her son's nature?

"He's what the Foundation would call a deviant."

"What?" Neff said, obviously astonished. "And... and you?"

Hannah shook her head. "He's adopted."

"You've kept him hidden here?"

"I had no choice. I found him abandoned by his parents, and a life of captivity is better than one spent haunting the woods until some hunter brings his head back into town."

Neff sat at the table, her face a mixture of fascination, fear and revulsion. Hannah found herself disappointed, but the young woman was a product of her conditioning, after all.

The doctor broke the silence. "So, there's something about his immune system that gives protection against viruses?"

"He's never had a day's sickness in all the time I've known him, even when I've come down with whatever virus is doing the rounds. I drew off a blood sample just before the Foundation rolled into town. When I got back from city hall, he was gone."

Neff regarded her closely. "What was the nature of his mutation? Was it obvious?"

"Let's put it this way," Hannah said. "He has the kind of face only a mother could love."

"And yet you did."

Tears emerged from the corners of Hannah's eyes. "I let him down. He's out there somewhere, alone and frightened. I should be looking."

"Why aren't you, then?" Lois said.

Hannah raised her hands as if gesturing to the world around her. "The plague came to town. I was going to go as soon as I could slip away, but the last thing I wanted to do was lead the Foundation to him. But yes, I should have gone. My first duty should have been to my son."

Lois nodded. "You know what your trouble is?"

"Enlighten me."

"You think you can do it all, have it all. You thought you could hide a mutant in your house *and* continue to live among normal people. You thought you could wait the Foundation out when he disappeared, and go fetch him, then, presumably, put him back in whatever cage you hid him in. Then the plague came, and Hannah Myers is the only person who can save everyone, so you forgot about your son. Tell me, when would you have gone after him?"

Hannah felt her jaw tighten like a vice. "When I could. And you're wrong. I don't try to have it all, because I've learned to my cost that when I do that, I end up with nothing. Yes, Roberto's my son, but this is my city and a couple of thousand lives depend on us getting the plague under control. Am I arrogant for thinking I was the right person to do it? Maybe, but there's two things you've got to know about me, Lois. First, I know my limitations, and I know how important it is to work with the right people, otherwise I promise you wouldn't be sitting at my table now.

"And remember this. I was there, Lois. I was there at the end of the world. I escaped the first wave by dumb luck and spent the next three months trying to warn the world about the second wave. Call me arrogant if you like, but the truth is, I know what the stakes are. I've seen what happens when people with knowledge of what's coming don't do what has to be done to help their fellow human beings. Because of me and my friends, tens of thousands survived the second wave rather than being burned to a crisp.

"So, excuse me if I don't always live up to your expectations, but when I die, which will be soon enough, I will go to my grave knowing I did my best for my species, even if it meant sacrificing everything that meant anything to me personally. Judge me if you like. Frankly, I no longer give a crap."

Silence settled on the kitchen as Hannah brought her breathing under control.

Then there was a knock on the door.

"Who the hell is that?" Ida had been the only person she'd seen in recent days, and she didn't bother to knock.

Lois sprung to her feet and strode over to the window which looked out over the front garden. "Oh my God."

Hannah had arrived at her shoulder to see two figures at the front door dressed in black suits. "What the hell?"

Then she recognized something familiar in the nearer figure, and her heart froze. "You called the Foundation?"

Lois swung around. "No! I swear!" She ran to the back door, but before she reached the handle, she saw the shadow of someone outside.

"Was this some kind of setup? Were they listening to my confession?"

"Honestly, Hannah. I don't know anything. I thought they'd gone!

"Well, they're back," Hannah spat as she headed for the door.

The familiar figure smiled at her from behind a filtered mask. He put his hand out to stop her stepping over the threshold, moved back a pace and lifted the mask half-off his face.

"Carver," she said.

He wagged a finger reproachfully. "Representative Carver. Decorum costs nothing, after all."

"What are you doing here?"

"Ah, I see Doctor Neff is also with you. Good. It seems you have made progress in finding a cure for the plague. That's excellent. The Foundation's facilities are the best in the world, and are at your disposal."

Hannah nodded, feeling like the mouse sniffing the cheese and looking for the trap.

"I'm surprised you're not more pleased, Doctor," Carver continued. "You and Doctor Neff now have the means to create a treatment for all."

"A treatment that will belong to the Foundation."

Carver shrugged. "Does that matter? Can you think of a more efficient means of distributing it than using us?"

"You'll use it to blackmail."

"Now, now, Doctor. Your flights of fancy really do get the better of you sometimes. But even if it were true, you will undeniably save more lives with our help."

"Do I have a choice?"

Again, the shrug. "We all have choices. I suggest you think very carefully before spurning our help."

"Or what?"

Carver shook his head, as if feeling genuine regret. "We know about Roberto."

Hannah spun around, arm swinging back. "You!"

"No!" Lois yelled, raising her hands.

"Stop!" Carver said, and Hannah froze. "Doctor Neff did not tell us of your mutant child. That honor went to Mayor Snider. Even now, my people are scouring the countryside looking for him and when he's found, his hope rests with you, Doctor Myers."

"You son of a bitch! There is no hope for him! If you find him, you'll kill him."

Carver said nothing, merely looking directly into Hannah's eyes. "The gene pool will be cleansed of this monstrosity, but there are many ways to die, and some are painless. And you know the punishment for harboring a mutant. Let me speak plainly. Help us or you both burn alive."

Chapter 32

GENE

REUBEN WATCHED WITH LITTLE hope as Mrs. Short worked on her husband. Frankly, he'd expected the man to be dead by the time he'd seen Macias loaded into the wagon that had carried Roberto and Burrell and driven away. He suspected that if the exciser ever found out that he'd been transported in the same space previously occupied by a mutant he'd have himself cleansed in an acid bath and Lieutenant Hobbs' head on a spike. Reuben said a prayer that Macias was already discovering at first hand where evil souls go when they die.

Howie had been found under one of the wagons, having crawled away with bruised ribs and a black eye to show for taking a shot at Gallo. The little man had brushed off his injuries, though he was in obvious pain, and was now helping Mrs. Short.

To his shame, Reuben had left them to it and gone in search of Lucifer, but Skeeter had caught up with him on his own mount leading the black horse. He'd been found in the woods having jettisoned the man who'd tried to steal him.

A wave of relief flooded through Reuben as he hugged his old friend's head, and he thanked Skeeter many times before returning to the wrecked caravan.

He found Gene Burrell lying beside Karl's wagon, leaning against the wheel, his arm around Roberto's shoulder. The other members of the convoy were sifting through the debris and lamenting their bad luck, and they were keeping their distance from the monster and his guardian.

Reuben knelt beside the old man. "How are you?"

"I've been better," he gasped, gesturing at his legs. His pants were blackened rags, ending in feet that were a livid red, with bulbous blisters breaking out along his shins.

"Is there anything I can do for you?"

Burrell grunted. "I'd welcome a bullet in the head."

"No!"

The boy, who'd been hugging Burrell's chest, jerked backward, revealing his monstrous face. Reuben was better prepared this time, but he still couldn't process what he was seeing. It was like a horror movie fan's badly made cosplay mask.

"Don't leave me," the boy said, stroking the old man's face.

Burrell forced a smile as he looked at the boy without a trace of repulsion. "Might not have a choice, son."

Then his eyes turned in Reuben's direction. "Will you see the boy back to his mom, if I can't? You did a fine thing standing up to that evil man. We'd both be dead now if you hadn't."

Reuben shook his head, wondering whether perhaps it would have been better for them both if they hadn't survived. Roberto had escaped without serious injury, but what kind of a future did he have in a world that would see him killed on sight if he ever left the shadows?

And Burrell himself was in agony. Reuben felt a mix of pity and guilt as he looked down at the old man. If he'd acted just a little quicker, maybe he could have spared him the worst of the pain. If he'd left it just a little longer, he'd have been beyond help and would be at peace now. As it was, Burrell inhabited a hinterland between life and death, too slowly walking the path from one to the other.

"Hello."

Reuben glanced up to see Asha, who held out a hand to Roberto, showing no sign of revulsion as he smiled at the mutant.

"You're very sad. I'm sorry."

Roberto's face shifted into what must have been a smile, though he then winced as his skin tore, forming fresh channels of livid red.

"Can you help my grandpa?"

Asha moved past Reuben to kneel beside Gene, taking the old man's hand. Burrell, who'd been lapsing into delirium, woke up, his pupils sharpening as he looked at the boy.

"Are you his grandpa?"

Burrell shook his head. "Not by... blood."

"I wish I had a grandpa like you. You're a good man."

"Thank... thank you, son."

"Are you in much pain?"

Reuben could see tears running down Burrell's cheeks as he gave a tiny nod.

"Then you can go, if you want. We'll look after Roberto."

"No!" the mutant cried,

Asha took the boy's fingers in his free hand, as if he acted as a link between the two of them. "It's okay. Sometimes it has to be like this."

"What are you doing?" Reuben said.

Asha glanced at him, face pale as death. "I'm trying to help. There is so much love, so much pain."

Reaching into his inside pocket, Reuben took out his roll of drugs, then found the remaining morphine dose he'd reserved for Lucifer, and put it in Burrell's hand. Asha was trying to calm Roberto, so he didn't see the exchange of understanding between the two men. Reuben gave Burrell a canteen of water and, without hesitation, Gene Burrell forced the narcotic down, swallowing deeply.

"Thank you," he whispered as Reuben leaned in,

"His mother, is it Hannah Myers?"

Burrell's eyes snapped open as if in fear.

"It's okay, I'm a friend," Reuben said. "I've come from the West to find her."

"She's in Mecklen," the old man said. "Take the boy to her."

Reuben nodded. "I will. Rest now in peace."

He sat back and watched the man relax. After a few minutes, Asha looked at Burrell. "He's gone," he said, letting the old man's hand go before drawing Roberto into an embrace as the mutant child howled.

REUBEN SAT BY THE campfire, sharing a bottle of liquor with Skeeter, and finally finding some peace. His only plan right now was to drink himself into the kind of deep sleep he certainly wouldn't get sober.

For now, all he sought was oblivion, so he'd awaken with a refreshed body even if his mind was still reeling from what had happened today.

Howie was snoring just behind them. He'd worked for hours with Mrs. Short to save her husband and, for now, it seemed they'd succeeded. Escalante had turned from being a burden who Reuben had intended to discard as soon as possible to a man of true value. If he hadn't shot at Gallo, then Reuben would likely be dead now, and Roberto would be ashes.

"What's eating you, Boss?" Skeeter said.

Another burden who'd turned out to be more than he appeared, Reuben had found comfort in Skeeter's uncomplicated nature. His simplistic view of life and the world was not realistic, but sometimes it exposed a kernel of truth, in the same way that a child's naivete can cut through the BS.

And Reuben had children on his mind. Roberto was one, and the greater practical problem if Reuben was to fulfill his promise to Burrell. But he wasn't the one Reuben was thinking of right now as he downed another shot of liquor.

"It's Asha."

"What about him?"

Reuben sighed. He knew the alcohol was loosening his tongue, but that didn't stop him.

"He's weird."

Skeeter laughed, causing heads to turn before the others resumed their own private conversations. "Well, he sure is. He's like an old man in a kid's body."

"Yeah. That's part of it, but it's more than that. I sometimes feel I'm in the presence of some kind of, I don't know..." His voice trailed off. Truth was, he couldn't put his finger on what bugged him, he just knew that something did.

"Like a little Buddha."

"How do you know about Buddha?"

Skeeter laughed again, then slapped his hand over his face. "My pa used to say 'If brains were dynamite, I wouldn't be able to blow my own nose' but I seen some things in my time. I seen baby Buddhas, though the one I saw had big ears and a face like a possum."

"That was Baby Yoda," Reuben said with a smile, enjoying a moment's reminiscence. "But it's much the same. And yeah, I guess that's it. And the kid seems to know what people are thinking without them saying a word."

Skeeter nodded. "It's like a kind of magic. Are all muteys like him?"

"No. He's got to be careful, though. If the wrong people get the idea there's something unusual about him ..."

"About who?"

Karl had approached without either of them noticing, and he dropped next to Reuben, sitting cross-legged in front of the fire.

"Macias," Reuben lied, jabbing Skeeter in the ribs.

Karl nodded. "He sure was a mean son of a bitch. I know it's a sin, but I hope he's met his maker, whoever that is."

"How's Short?"

"Hard to say," Karl said, his face dropping. "Al's a fighter, and so is Josie. She won't let him give up but, you know, there's only so much she can do. Your friend Howie's done at least as much to help him. Assuming his stuff works."

Reuben smiled. "Worked on my shoulder. Well, it didn't kill me, at least. But look, I'm sorry about your caravan."

"It's okay. We'll pick ourselves up. I mean, I got plenty of grief from the waggoners, but when it comes down to it, it's going to be safer to travel together than apart. I guess, when they think about it, they know we were lucky to get away with our lives. They could have saved a ton of trouble if they'd just shot the lot of us and blamed it on bandits."

Reuben nodded. "Yeah, but it grinds my gears that they got away with it."

"There's always karma."

"Well, I wouldn't want to be in Hobbs' boots. As soon as they can find another dandy, they'll put a bullet through his brain."

Reuben poured a shot into Karl's glass. "What's next, then?"

"Well, we'll have to bury the dead in the morning. Hopefully Al Short won't be among them. Then I'll be heading to Harrisburg. Anyone who wants to come along is welcome. Then we'll start picking up the pieces. How about you?"

Draining his glass, Reuben felt a wave of exhaustion approaching. "I'm heading for Mecklen. Got a woman to find. I've got someone I think she'll be happy to see."

EPILOGUE

DESMOND MYERS SAT BESIDE Bella Sotto in her ancient, militarized Silverado as it rattled and belched its way along the highway. She'd made good progress with repurposing old cooking oil into fuel, but it was a far from perfect formulation.

"I don't know why I retired," Myers said, gripping the handrail. "If Bob's gonna call me up every time Otis can't decide whether to have his eggs plain or sunny-side up, then I might as well have stayed in the town hall."

"You won't get an argument from me. Bob only got elected because there was no one else stupid enough to want the job."

They halted at the north gate, a barrier made of recycled steel that was one of only three ways into the town of New Haven. Built in the years following the fall of humanity, it was the city's most visible achievement in those early days.

Desmond climbed down from the truck and strode toward the metal steps that led up to the top of the wall. He could barely keep his hand wrapped around the safety rail, the metal was so hot, but he finally made it to the walkway.

Crouching figures pointed their assault rifles down at a Jeep that had stopped twenty yards from the gate.

"What's occurring, Bob?"

Mayor Bob Riggs turned and nodded. "We've got a situation and the sheriff recommended we seek the benefit of your experience." He talked as if he had a mouthful of sand.

Sheriff Otis Boyd got to his feet and put down his rifle. "I'm glad you're here Mr. M — Myers. This Jeep arrived a half hour ago. Man inside, injured. Haven't heard nothing from him since he called out for help."

"So why haven't we sent a medic out to him?"

Boyd pointed down at the vehicle. "You see those markings?"

Desmond shielded his eyes and tried to focus on the Jeep. The first thing that struck him was that it looked relatively new. Sure, it was caked with dust, but otherwise it could have been built a week ago. Which was, of course, impossible.

The second thing he noticed was the device painted onto its roof and both doors. "Good grief. A shark."

"I figured that was just a rumor," Soto said, appearing beside him.

The shark was the motif of the North American Freedom Corps, a unit that had been formed in Washington State soon after the fall. Desmond had received occasional communications from them over the years, but they'd confined themselves to securing and administering the area around Seattle.

More recently, however, he'd heard that their commander had begun to expand their sphere of influence and, if the rumors were to be believed, he'd resorted to extreme violence against any who opposed him.

That, at least, explained the mystery of the new looking military vehicle parked outside their gate. It had somehow survived the repeated EMPs that had accompanied the auroras.

He spotted movement in the driver's seat of the Jeep. "Look, the guy needs our help. Seems to me that's our first concern."

"What if the rumors are true?" Mayor Riggs said.

"Which rumors, exactly? I've heard all kinds of stories lately."

The sheriff gestured at the car. "Plague. Word is they're using biological weapons."

"What do you think?" Desmond said to Bella Soto. "Is it credible?"

"I want to say no, Des, but what if they found a cache of biological weapons where they found that vehicle? If that's been in use for thirty-five years, then I'm a monkey's uncle."

Desmond sighed. "You know our rule, Bel."

"'No friend is denied entry.' But we don't know if he's a friend, do we?"

"Remember the last time we had a situation like this?"

"With the exciser? Sure, and I haven't forgotten what I said you should do with him."

"Remember what I actually did? Worked out okay, didn't it?"

Sotto chuckled. "I don't know why you ask me, Des. You're gonna do your own thing."

"Send me down with a first aid kit," Desmond said. "I'll drive him to the Olsen's place and do my best to treat him."

Bob Riggs went to protest or, at least, pretended to, but then said, "Well, if that's your recommendation..."

"It's okay, Bob, I won't blame you if I catch the plague from this guy."

He climbed down and waited at the gate. "Open it up," he called out.

Sotto stood beside him. "I'm coming with you."

"Good."

"Aren't you going to try to stop me?"

"Wouldn't dream of it. Anyway, would there be any point?"

"No. Your driving's so bad he'll probably die in an RTA than whatever's ailing him."

He slapped his old friend on the back and waited as the gate swung open.

DESMOND STRAIGHTENED HIMSELF AND rubbed his back before wiping the sweat from his brow. Then he took in a deep breath and began shoveling more sand out through the broken kitchen window.

He remembered Abel Olsen from before the fall. The old man would have had a fit to see his home being slowly swallowed by the desert. Back then, the sand kept itself to itself and was mainly confined to the east of here. Since the auroras, however, the world had dried, and the deserts had expanded.

The Olsen's farm had been abandoned decades before, the deep wells that fed the pivots having dried up and the discs of green now swallowed by the dust. But the barns here had been used to store equipment and harvest surpluses for many years and so the farmhouse had been kept in one piece until the grasshopper plague and the end of big surpluses.

"You should take a break," Sotto said, appearing in the doorway. "You'll slice your foot off if you're not careful."

They'd been taking turns to dig out the sand after the sun went down while the other tended the patient. They'd dragged a mattress into the basement as it was the coolest place in the house, and done their best to make him comfortable.

"How's he doing?"

"No change. Sometimes I think he's gonna wake up and then he just goes back into a deeper sleep."

"No sign of the plague though."

Sotto chuckled. "Huh. No. The only thing wrong with him is the bullet that was lodged in his back."

"He'll make it. I didn't think so when I first saw him in the Jeep, but he's got a hell of a constitution. If anyone can survive that amount of blood loss, it's him."

She took the shovel from him and handed him a bottle of water. "You take yourself downstairs and I'll finish here."

Desmond didn't argue, swigging the water and heading down the wooden steps of the basement.

The man was looking up at him.

"Glad to see you awake," Desmond said, hiding his surprise.

"Am I in New Haven?" the man responded, fatigue obvious in his voice. He was a tall, well-built man in his mid-twenties, and he'd been wearing an olive and tan combat uniform when they'd driven him here. The jacket hung over the back of a chair, a wide, uneven area of dark red covering the lower half.

Desmond sat down beside the bed, keeping his hand on the gun in his pocket. "Not exactly. This is an abandoned farm outside the town walls."

The soldier nodded wearily. "Smart. Thank you for not killing me on sight or leaving me to die."

"You're welcome. Now for some introductions, my name is Desmond Myers and I was the mayor of New Haven. Retired now, but sometimes I wonder. Now, the patch on your uniform just says X-16 which I guess is your designation. Are you special forces?"

The man's head rocked back, and he let out a laugh. "Well, yes, I suppose so. And X-16 is my designation, and my name."

"What was your birth name?" Desmond asked, thinking that he must have misunderstood.

"X-16."

Desmond scratched his head and decided to try a different tack. "So, where are you from?"

"JBLM-Lewis-McChord. Seattle."

"Your commanding officer?"

16's face stiffened. "General Reid."

"This is Specialist Sotto," Desmond said as she appeared at the bottom of the stairs, handgun leveled on the soldier.

Sotto stood at the foot of the bed. "Two questions. Why are you so far south? And who shot you?"

"Straight to the point, Bel."

"You know me. I like a story as much as anyone, but mysteries frustrate me."

X-16 pulled himself up a little then twisted, his fingers searching the bandages on his back. "You took out the bullet?"

"We did," Sotto responded. "Frankly, if Des here hadn't said otherwise, I'd have left you to die."

"How long have I been here?"

"Three days."

Desmond could see that he was making a calculation. "And no one else like me has appeared?"

"Nope. We got radio comms, and I'd have heard by now."

X-16 nodded. "Then I can answer your questions, though you probably won't believe me."

"Try us."

"I am a genetically engineered soldier, second generation. I was recently cast out of the program and if my sergeant hadn't tipped me off, I'd be dead by now."

"Why were you rejected?"

He shrugged. "I hesitated to fire on a civilian when ordered."

A wave of shock froze Desmond for a moment. "You were told to shoot a civilian?"

"That isn't the important part, Mr. Myers. I was on a raid and my comrades all performed flawlessly. The general intends to take the country. His only weakness is lack of manpower. So, he has engineered a plague variant that he uses to bring places under his control. For strategically important targets, he has the Sharks."

"The unit you were a member of?"

X-16 nodded.

"What's so special about them? I mean, they're special forces, but how much damage could they do? How many of them are there?"

"Twenty."

"Is that all?"

He shrugged. "It's enough to bring down a government or take a city. You don't know them, but I do. They have no compassion, no empathy, no hesitation, and they're trained from birth to become the ultimate soldiers."

This sounded like the ravings of a madman to Desmond. He had no doubt the soldier believed what he was saying, but that didn't make it true.

"I escaped and headed south, but they caught up with me."

"The Sharks?"

He chuckled. "No. The general doesn't waste them on tracking a worthless fugitive. He sent a squad of rangers after me. They caught up with me just south of Wendover."

"And that's where you got the wound?" Sotto asked.

"Yeah."

"So they could be after you still?"

"No."

Desmond looked into his eyes. "You killed them all?"

He saw nothing change in X-16's expression, no sign of regret, sadness or guilt. "Yes. I didn't have a choice."

"The man who shot you?"

"He was the last to die. Then I took their Jeep and came here."

"So, it was just luck that you ended up in New Haven?"

"No. I was heading here. Folks talk about this place, though most don't know where it is. Took some figuring out, but I asked around in Wendover and they said it was south of there. And they were right."

Desmond leaned forward and looked him in the eye. "Why did you come here?"

"Because the general killed my family, and he's gonna come here one day."

"So, it's all about revenge? Why should we help you?" Sotto asked.

"Because I'm the only son of a bitch who knows how to fight the Sharks. Now, you can either have me on your side or send me on my way and face them alone. All I ask is you leave the general to me."

Desmond looked up at Sotto. "We'll have to think about this. We don't have the power to agree, even if we wanted to. For now, you should concentrate on getting well. Either way, you're going to need your strength."

Pain lanced across X-16's face. "You got any morphine? Anything like that?"

Sotto went across to the med kit and found the bottle.

Desmond watched X-16 as he reached out for the pill. And he instantly knew how the general controlled his creations. The only emotion X-16 had shown was the yearning of addiction. He'd used a matter-of-fact monotone to describe how he'd killed an entire squad. No pride, no guilt, nothing. He was like a machine, albeit one with a fault, and Desmond's imagination conjured up an image of flint-faced terminators striding south.

They were coming.

WHAT HAPPENS NEXT

Thank you for reading *Into the Dark*, the second
book in the *Future's Fall* series.
The story continues in the next instalment: Over the
Edge (https://books2read.com/futuresfall3), I hope
you'll join me on this post apocalyptic adventure.
Kev Partner

WHAT HAPPENED BEFORE

The events in this book take place thirty-five years after those of the Nightfall series. If you haven't read it yet, you can get the complete series in one edition for pennies here: The Complete Nightfall (https://books2read.com/NightfallComplete).

Future's Fall is its own story, and independent of *Nightfall*, but if you like the book you've just completed, you'll enjoy its precursor series. And you'll meet some familiar characters.

Free Story and More from Me

Fancy a free post apocalyptic story? Click here to download Final Justice (https://scrib.me/finaljusti ce), the first appearance of John Hunter, judge, jury and executioner.

And here's where you can find more from me:

Website: www.kevpartner.co.uk

Library: books2read.com/rl/kevpartner

Follow me on Bookbub: www.bookbub.com/au thors/kevin-partner

Facebook: www.fb.com/KevPartnerAuthor

Made in the USA
Coppell, TX
27 December 2022

90832156R00148